Once Upon a Punchline

HOLLY SCHINDLER

Holly Schindler's
comedies:

Funny Meeting You Here
Funny You Should Mention That

Check HollySchindler.com
for details and to sign up for her comedy newsletter.

Table of Contents

once upon a punchline

The Storyteller

MOST important people arrive on horses, colors flying, trumpets blaring.

This guy came on roller skates, playing a kazoo.

Oh, and he had on a helmet. Like you usually wear on a bicycle or a skateboard. Which was pretty good indication he wasn't all that skillful on the skates.

"Gather 'round!" he exclaimed, his wheels thunking on the boardwalk.

But since most of the people within earshot could also see the skates and could hear the kazoo he was blaring all over again, they snorted and dismissed him.

Besides, it was a sunny, beautiful day. Everyone was enjoying shave ice and shade trees. Shoes were kicked off. The air smelled of sunscreen. Dogs were rolling in the grass. Didn't this guy know the laziest days were the ones in which no one had any time to spare on such nonsense?

"Adulting is *hard*!" he announced.

Now, that got everybody's attention.

It *was* hard.

"But so was childhood!" he went on.

At this point, he started to lose them again.

"Now, now," he said. "I know you aren't fools. You

remember your childhoods. Why, they'd been so simple. Compared to parenting and pandemics and careers and mortgages, anyway. What you wouldn't give to go back!"

A few edged forward, because he was speaking their language once more. It was a little hesitant, though, because now they were seeing the guy had Scam Artist written all over him. I mean, literally—somebody at the last place he'd been had actually tacked a sign on his back that said just that: "SCAM ARTIST," in giant letters. When he raised his arms, the sign crinkled, tipping him off. He frowned and flapped around a bit, trying to get hold of it. When he finally grasped the bottom corner, he gave it a good yank. He frowned at the message.

Then he balled up the sheet of paper and tossed it over his shoulder.

"In childhood—which you all remember so fondly," he began, "didn't we tell over-the-top stories, set in ridiculous 'magical' kingdoms?" He was sure to put some exaggerated air quotes around *magical* as he spoke. "Didn't we enjoy those less-than-serious messengers? We didn't dismiss them! Nobody ever put 'SCAM ARTIST' on the backs of the Brothers Grimm. Of course not. We loved them. Thought they were storytelling masters. What happened to that?

"How did everyone get so suspicious?" he went on. "It didn't used to be that way. I'm no snake oil salesman! I'm not trying to sell you anything at all. I thought we'd have a fun afternoon. Sheesh."

Everyone began to sneak guilty side-eyes at one another. They had all been judging this particular storyteller every bit as harshly as whoever had taped that sign to his back. Really, though, he did have a point. What was scammy about him? Why were they so ready to dismiss him?

It wasn't like he'd promised to help settle their debt or had claimed to be a prince needing help transferring funds. He hadn't asked for a single social security number, date of birth, or blood type. Somewhere along the way, they'd all turned distrustful of kazoos? Why? The cynicism made them feel crummy—like they'd soured somehow—grown a bit of back-of-the-fridge funk right over their once-pure hearts.

"Didn't we love the wild tales of our youth, delight in them?" he asked them all. "Wasn't a good bedtime story one of our most favorite parts of childhood?"

Slowly, heads began to nod.

"Then why not explore adulting in the same way?" he asked. "In fact," he went on, tugging a book out of thin air, "I have such a volume right here. Filled with fairy tales and bedtime stories set in magical kingdoms. All meant to explore—with a smile and a wink—the rough waters of…

adulting."

He cracked the book open and began to read…

Freewheeling

O nce upon a time, on the planet of Yeahright, just to the left of the planets of Yagottabekidding and Nobodybelievesthat, Spoke Ann was but a spoke in a wheel. Timmy Thompson's bicycle wheel, to be exact. All her life she'd been a spoke. She'd been born a spoke to spoke parents. Her brothers and sisters and aunts and uncles were spokes. Growing up, her teachers had been spokes. Her friends and neighbors were also spokes. Her boss was a spoke. Her boyfriend was a spoke. It was so hard to meet someone who wasn't on your own wheel. And even if you did—what kind of future was there in it?

Secretly, Spoke Ann longed to be on her own. Okay, it wasn't that secret. On bright cheery mornings, she would always wake crying out, "I'm so tired of moving in circles!" And, "I'd give anything to be free! Free from the wheel! Free to go where I want, whenever I want!"

So that was a pretty big tip-off.

But, as is the case on the planet of Yeahright, wishes had a way of coming true, out of nowhere.

One bright and very cheery morning—the kind of morning during which only the grumpiest of grumps could continue to grump—Timmy Thompson decided to practice bicycle tricks in a paved lot next to a grassy park.

If you've been wondering about Timmy, I should tell you he's a large dose of *lovely young man* with a splash of *wonder-what-would-happen-if-you-put-a-firecracker-in-this-hole-and-lit-it.*

So, you know, a normal kid.

Anyway, he was out there practicing tricks. He'd forgotten that he was not supposed to wear his new shirt. For some reason, mothers tended to think that new shirts were not for wearing. What's the deal with that, anyway? You buy the shirt because the old ones look crummy, but then you get mad because I wear the new one?

There's not a kid who hasn't thought that—usually while getting reamed because the new shirt is already covered in ketchup and paint from the fence they forgot not to lean up against and has a burned spot created when they found out what would happen if you put a lit firecracker in that hole over there on Fourth and Elm.

All before being seen in the shirt by their classmates and teacher.

That's the kicker, isn't it? The shirt needs to be seen by somebody in charge. Because, really, that's all a parent can do. Ship kids off looking decent. *See?* new, clean shirts say when they walk through school entrances. *I, the parent of this child, have done my job. Maybe that'll score me some extra points when he does whatever he's going to do on the playground today, because let's face it, eight-year-olds are far less predictable than the lottery. Most of us are better off taking our chances with the bulls in Pamplona.*

Anyway, there Timmy was, skidding through puddles and popping wheelies and spraying gravel.

Which was another thing: if Spoke Ann had to be a spoke, why couldn't she be a spoke on a bicycle wheel that belonged to an artist in France? Each morning, said artist could take her bike outside to engage in a little plein air painting. Now, *that* would be lovely. As it was, though, she was stuck on a kid's bike.

The embarrassment.

It was almost too much to bear.

As Timmy's front tire raced toward a giant yellow speed bump, Spoke Ann's father warned, "Hang on!"

But Spoke Ann grinned, seeing her chance. When the bike crashed against the speed bump, Spoke Ann let go.

"Yeeeeeaaaaaaaahhhh! Weeee ouuuuuuuaaahhh eurrraasgh!" she shouted. Or something to that effect. And soared into the air. It was such a beautiful feeling, finally being free. Like breaking up with your whole life.

She came down softly in the grass at the edge of the lot.

Timmy wobbled left, right, then left again. "Noooooooo!" he shouted, flopping over to the side, skinning his knee.

"Oh, this is terrible!" he said, seeing the mud and the hole along the bottom of his new shirt. "Oh, I'm going to be murdered!" He stood, suddenly angry. "You stupid bike! What's wrong with you? You never sway back and forth like that. Now, look what you made me do."

He righted the bike and walked it down the street. Spoke Ann giggled at the way he was practicing his limp, clearly hoping that when he got home, he'd get more sympathy for his skinned knee than anger over his wrecked new shirt.

"When I woke up this morning, I never would have imagined that I'd be completely free before the afternoon was over!" Spoke Ann shouted. She smiled, happier than she'd ever been.

Soon, the grass beneath her made her itch. But Spoke Ann didn't have arms, and she couldn't scratch.

When the clouds slid past, the sun blared straight into her eyeballs, turning her corneas into those crispy burned bits on the bottom of a frying pan.

"Sure would be nice to get out of this spot for a while," Spoke Ann said. But she didn't have legs, and she couldn't stand up. "Oh, no!" Spoke Ann cried out. "If I can't walk, how am I supposed to get *anywhere*?" She felt sick, suddenly.

Really, though, it was to be expected. Not to rely on stereotypes or anything, but spokes are not exactly great planners.

"What do we have here?" The pink head of an earthworm emerged from the dark space between two blades of grass.

"I've jumped off my wheel, and now I'm stranded!" Spoke Ann explained.

"That's a sad story," the earthworm said. "I can't imagine what kind of life a spoke could ever hope to have without a wheel. But I can't help you. I really must get out of the way of that lawnmower." He burrowed deep into the ground.

A giant black wheel rolled straight for Spoke Ann's head. She closed her eyes and gritted her teeth. "Goodbye, cruel world!" she shouted.

But the lawnmower stopped, and a warm hand plucked her from the grass. When she opened her eyes, Spoke Ann was looking straight into a stubble-covered face.

"Am I glad to see you, sir!" she shouted, as though they were long-lost friends. Like they'd gone to college together or something. When, in truth, Spoke Ann had never seen this man in her life. "I live on Timmy Thompson's wheel. Do you know him?"

But the groundskeeper couldn't hear her over the mower. "This spoke could have ruined my new blade," he complained. He made a motion as though to toss Spoke Ann over his shoulder, but stopped. If he threw her, she could *still* destroy his blade.

He put her in the pocket of his jacket, which smelled of breath mints and cigarettes and dirt. She spent the entire day there, going from one lawn to another, and knowing that she was getting increasingly farther from home. To make matters worse, the groundskeeper was also something of a rock collector. He kept putting interesting stones in his jacket pocket, which kept whacking Spoke Ann in the head. She felt a little like a ping-pong paddle.

The groundskeeper knocked off at the end of the day, and he went to a bar. Spoke Ann knew it was a bar because the groundskeeper made some crack at the door about no one wanting his ID anymore. The place smelled funny—sad and a little desperate. Were all bars sad? At times, Timmy had leaned his bike against the wall of his house, and Spoke Ann had been able to watch a little TV through the living room window. On TV, bars seemed like wonderful places, where there was singing and partying and love was found.

Was that a lie? What other things about the outside world had also been lies?

When the groundskeeper stuck his hand in his pocket, looking for his cigarettes, he found Spoke Ann.

"Hey," he said, pulling her out. "Whaddaya know? Guess I can safely toss you now."

"Wait!" Spoke Ann cried out. "I can do things. Really! I could—Oooh! I hear there are poles that dance. Isn't that right? Don't bars have pole dancers? I could be one—I mean, I'm practically a pole myself. Is that self-exploitation? I think I could be good at that! Or—or—I'm so skinny, I could sell diet supplements. Would that be exploiting other people? Making money off insecurities I tell them they should have? Is it more noble to exploit yourself?

"And listen, whatever happens, I'll need you to get me to work and back and take me home with you every night. I'd pay you for your trouble. I'm just a helpless spoke out here. Surely you won't abandon me."

But that's exactly what he did. He tossed Spoke Ann.

"Whhhhhhooooooooaaaaa!" she screamed, sailing through the air. "Eeeueuuueueaaaaahh!" Or something to that effect. Where would she land next? "Not the water!"

She sank to the bottom of a nearby fountain, next to the pennies and nickels that had been tossed in with all the wishes.

What was the deal with that, anyway? Why were people always wishing with money? Did they think they needed to pay for a wish? Why—to make it come true? Were they trying to bribe whatever invisible *thing* was out there in charge of wishes coming true? Or did they think they needed to pay for the privilege of wishing? Spoke Ann had made a wish earlier that day, and it had been granted—just like that. No payment involved.

Lucky her.

"Help! Somebody!" Spoke Ann begged. Bubbles traveled from her mouth to the surface of the water.

Spoke Ann could make out a hazy boy's face.

"Timmy?" she pleaded.

Only, it wasn't. It was just some random kid who had come by to scoop up all the change; that fountain money funded his vending machine candy habit.

(See? Spending money on wishes is foolish. Foolish! It just gets turned into some kid's Hot Tamales and gummy worms.)

"You've saved me!" she shouted.

But she wasn't quite sure that was the case anymore when he ran to a nearby neighborhood, pressed her head against a chain-link fence, and took off running.

Her head throbbed as she bounced against the fence. "Stop!" she begged. Oh, how she missed Timmy. "Wu-wu-ow-owow!" she bellowed. Or, you know, something to *that* effect.

But the boy *didn't* stop—not until a distant mother's voice called her son home to dinner. Then, he paused, at least.

He had just started taking off again when he discovered his shoe was untied. He dropped Spoke Ann and turned his attention to his shoelace. By the time he reknotted it, he'd already forgotten about her. He took off again, skipping, blissfully unaware of how lucky he really was to be able to skip.

Spoke Ann began to sob.

"What's wrong?" a smiling yellow dandelion asked.

"I decided I'd had enough of my wheel." Spoke Ann sniffed. "So I jumped off to be free."

"You don't look like you're enjoying your freedom."

"I'm not," Spoke Ann admitted. "But I was so tired of going in circles."

"What's so bad about that?" the dandelion asked. "I never get to go anywhere. My feet are underground," she said, pointing toward her roots. "But my entire dandelion family is here. I have plenty of sun and rain."

"On my wheel, I was never lonely," Spoke Ann lamented. "And Timmy did a pretty good job of keeping us warm and dry in the garage. I mean, he might have forgotten a time or two, but here, I'm alone and afraid."

"You can stay here with me," the dandelion offered, patting Spoke Ann with one of her leaves.

There, Spoke Ann spent a long and lonely night.

In the morning, under the harsh glow of daybreak, a shadow trailed across Spoke Ann. She could tell from the expression on the dandelion's face that she was in danger. She couldn't bear to look.

A gush of wind washed over her as she was lifted into the air. When she sneaked a peek, Spoke Ann realized she was inside a bluebird's beak. They flew a long way, it seemed, all the way to a half-built nest in a redbud tree.

Spoke Ann began to cry again. She didn't want to become part of a bluebird's nest. "I want to go home!" she wailed.

Seeing some better building material under a maple tree, the bluebird opened her beak. Spoke Ann tumbled through the air.

She was too tired and upset and gloomy to make so much as a peep.

This time, she hit a pile of blond hair and fell to the ground.

The blond-haired boy squatted to pick her up.

"Timmy!" Spoke Ann shouted. "What a relief!"

"You're telling me!" Timmy raced to the bike lying in the grass. "I've been looking for you since yesterday! This back wheel has been useless without you."

"Spoke Ann!" the rest of the spokes cried out as Timmy wedged her into her old spot. "You're back!"

"I'd jump for joy if I could," Spoke Ann admitted.

"What happened to you?" they asked.

"I jumped from the wheel. I wanted to be free. I wanted to be on my own."

"That's a silly thing to wish for," Timmy told her.

"It is!" Spoke Ann agreed. "And now I know—now I realize—we're all kind of spokes in a wheel. Aren't we? I mean, we all have things we have to do, things that can make us feel a little like we all just fit some slot in somebody else's agenda, their plan. You know?"

"Actually—no. I don't—" Timmy started, but Spoke Ann didn't let him finish his thought.

"I mean, I bet you feel like you have no say in where you go or what you do," Spoke Ann said. "Your parents are always making you go to school and the dentist. They make you comb your hair and go to bed. And it's not just your parents—it's also your teachers and the crossing guards and librarians and your older sister.

"And listen, kid, if you think you've got it bad..." Spoke Ann let out a whistle. "I'm an adult. I know how it is. Once you're grown, you don't get to call the shots, either. Your parents have to pay taxes and be at boring work meetings on time. Heck, if you mess up, you sit in the principal's office. Your parents mess up, they're going to the hoosegow!"

"Man, Spoke Ann, this is depressing."

"Yeah!" chimed in the rest of the spokes.

"Yeah!" echoed a nearby bird.

"Yeah!" the groundskeeper repeated. (Look, I have no idea where that groundskeeper came from—maybe he felt bad about tossing Spoke Ann out, abandoning her in her time of need. Who knows?)

"Yeah!" said the earthworm. "Depressing!"

"But, no, don't you see?" Spoke Ann asked. "It's wrong to feel that way! That's not true. The thing is, we're all meant for something. A job that fits us like nothing else. We can get so lost in thinking adventure has to be something new. But it's not—adventure is doing what you're meant to do. Being depended on. We need earthworms to chomp up organisms and fungi in the ground, so the soil can grow grass, so the groundskeeper over there has a job, so he can spend money at the sad bar!"

"That seems a little depressing, too, come to think of it," Timmy said.

"No, no—having a place in life—isn't that what it's all about? Needing each other—depending on each other—that's what makes the world *go 'round*!"

Again, not to be stereotypical about it, but spokes are known for their abilities with wordplay and puns.

"I felt strong, too, being your spoke," Spoke Ann went on. "But all I did was complain. We're meant to be together. You, me, and the rest of the spokes on the bike."

"Yes!" Timmy exclaimed. "I feel that way too! And I know exactly what fits me. What I want to do."

"Oh, yeah? What's that?"

"I'm going to be a BMX freestyle competitor."

"A what?"

"You know—360 tailwhips and heel clickers and bunny hops and fishtails and cannonballs!"

"Wait. What?"

"Oh, yeah," Timmy said, righting his bike—which, now that Spoke Ann looked, actually was a BMX bike. "I've been playing it safe until now. But we're going to get started on the hardcore tricks today. Just wait. You and me, we'll be flying through the air and spinning and flipping upside down in no time. This'll be a bigger adventure than you could ever imagine."

"Wait. Wait. Timmy," Spoke Ann begged. "Is there room for negotiation? Have you ever heard of plein air painting? Timmy!"

The Power of the Smile & Nod

Once upon *another* time, there was a young boy named Julian. On the day Julian turned eighteen, he was presented with a long velvet box. His first thought was that he hoped it was a hot dog. Julian loved hot dogs like he loved little else. He was, in fact, a hot dog connoisseur. He had never seen a hot dog come presented in a velvet box, but there was, as they say, a first time for everything. Maybe, he thought, really good gourmet hot dogs were frequently presented in velvet boxes.

When he creaked the box open, though, he was quite disappointed to find that inside lay nothing but a piece of paper.

"Rats," he grumbled.

"Why, Julian," his father proclaimed, "don't you realize what that is?"

Julian sighed, removed the slip of paper from the box, and held it up to the light. "It appears to be a ticket to Toxic Masculinity."

"Yes! Well, actually, it's more like a gift card, but I like the way you put it. A ticket to Toxic Masculinity." His father started to jump, but frowned, crossed his arms over his chest, and admitted, "I thought you'd be more excited."

"To go to a place called Toxic Masculinity?" Julian asked, his top lip raised off his teeth.

"Well, when my friends and I turned eighteen, we couldn't wait to get there."

Still, Julian stared with that Elvis lip of his.

"Different times, I suppose," his father said.

Julian felt bad. He could tell by the droop in his father's shoulders that he had anticipated this would be something the two of them could share.

"Well, I should give it a shot, at least," Julian relented.

His father's eyes brightened. "I'm so glad! Hurry on now," he added, slamming Julian's ballcap on his head and pushing him out the door. "I'll be here when you get back. I want to hear all about it."

"Don't you want to come?" Julian asked.

This made his father tilt his head in that way of his, indicating this had touched him. His cheeks turned Santa-Claus-pink. "I would love nothing more," he admitted.

His father jumped behind the wheel and the two of them took off. "This ol' car could drive out there on autopilot," his father admitted. "I've been going to Toxic Masculinity for years! Nothing like the first time you get to walk through that door, though."

Julian wasn't so sure.

As he'd feared, Toxic Masculinity was located in the older section of town, the side that used to house the discotheques and the cafeteria-style restaurants. A yellowed sign in a bar window advertised two-for-one Harvey Wallbangers. The whole block was looking a little shabby, frankly. And there were plenty of parking spaces open all down the curb.

Julian had passed down this street plenty of times, always

on his way somewhere else. Actually, he hadn't been aware that Toxic Masculinity was even in existence. For a moment, he wondered if his father'd gotten it all wrong, and the place had gone out of business years ago. But, no, as they drove, there it suddenly was, appearing out of nowhere, as though it had been dropped down from the sky: Toxic Masculinity. In neon, no less.

"Oh, boy!" his dad shouted.

Julian started to snort a laugh. But he sucked it back in when he realized his dad was being serious.

Julian stepped onto the sidewalk, taking deep breaths and bracing himself for whatever waited for him. Why did he agree to this?

The salesclerk on the other side of the glass appeared to do something akin to a touchdown dance. She raced to the entrance and held it open for Julian.

"Come in, come in!" she cooed.

The salesclerk was what Julian's father would have described as *all dolled up*. She had bouffant dyed blond hair and a shirt that showed off plenty of cleavage. She kept smiling at Julian with her glittery lips and adjusting her outfit like she wanted him to notice it.

Julian was not really all that great at compliments. They came out sounding clunky and insincere. So he just smiled and nodded. He considered the combo smile and nod move to be highly underrated, as it could be used in a variety of situations and to say a multitude of different things. For example, right now, it was a compliment. But at school, after dropping his books on Farrah Fitzweather's foot, it was an apology. And at home, when his father was nagging him about his curfew, it was an agreement to be back on time. In the principal's office or when being addressed by his boss, it was a *yes, sir*. It was never sarcastic or misinterpreted.

He often wondered why the smile and nod combo was

not in the How to Respond to All Situations Hall of Fame.

The salesclerk wore a name tag that identified her as Sandra, and she cocked her head at the smile and nod. Julian had pleased her.

See? Julian wanted to tell his father. *It works.*

The other thing about Sandra, Julian began to realize, was that she was old. With lots and lots of wrinkles, the kind his grandmother'd had all over her at her ninety-seventh birthday. Sandra was kind of a cross, Julian thought, between a Golden Girl and a Bond Girl.

Julian's father drifted off to the side. But not before he and Sandra exchanged a knowing look. Probably, Julian thought, he and Sandra had been on a first-name basis for years. Anyway, the look said they were going to let the kid handle this one all on his own.

"Cigarette?" she asked Julian, opening a gold case.

"I don't smoke," Julian told her.

"No one does anymore," Sandra said, disappointed. Apparently, she had herself been using the offer to light other people's cigarettes in the same way Julian used the smile and nod.

Julian decided to get this show on the road. He handed her his ticket.

Sandra gasped. "You must be eighteen today!"

"I am."

"This is special. Come right this way."

Julian could still not make heads or tails of this place, and he could glean no new information when Sandra pressed a button on the far wall. An entire section of said wall slid open and a giant clothes rack popped out. Garments started flying past at approximately fifty-seven miles per hour.

It was little more than a complete blur.

Julian scratched his head.

"Not sure which one you want?" Sandra asked.

"Remember, that welcome-to-manhood coupon of yours entitles you to a free one of your choice."

"What are they?"

"Why, capes, of course!" his father butted in. He shrugged at Sandra in a way that said, *Kids! What can you do?*

It seemed to embarrass him that Julian didn't know this. But how could he?

Julian did have a faint memory of coming upon his father's collection of capes. It had been years ago. Had to be more than ten. He hadn't been able to resist the large pieces of fabric, all folded up neatly in the back of his parents' closet. The one he'd tugged free had "SUPER DAD" branded across it. He'd tried to turn it into a fort using kitchen chairs, and his father had gotten uncharacteristically angry. "You'll learn about such things when you're old enough," he had scolded, folding the cape and returning it to the closet.

In the end, there had been a bit of shame in finding the capes. Almost like finding an assortment of prophylactics in the nightstand in the master bedroom, even though everyone knew what went on in there.

Julian also knew there were still old-timers who wore capes. He couldn't imagine how horribly uncomfortable it must be to wear a cape underneath your clothes. Most of the guys Julian knew had long ago gleefully tossed them aside, the same way previous generations had tossed undershirts or those weird garter things that used to hold up socks.

And another thing: how often had any of these old-school devotees ever stumbled upon situations in which their oh-so-precious capes had actually come in handy? Julian's grandfather had told him the story (over and over and over again) of placing—with the grandest of flourishes, mind you—his own cape over a puddle for a lovely young lady to walk across. (Said lady, of course, later became Julian's grandmother.) It had never been laundered, in order to preserve every detail of the once-in-a-lifetime encounter, and was still soiled with vintage mud.

Yes, Julian had long been aware of all this. But no one had ever told him capes—and this Toxic Masculinity place—were going to be part of his own life.

"There are capes here for every stage of life," his dad assured him. "It's getting the right first one that can be so tricky."

Julian was getting a bit sick to his stomach. It was beginning to dawn on him that simply buying one of these things was never going to satisfy his father. He'd expect Julian to wear it, which would quite possibly result in terminal ribbing from his friends. The thing would never even fold up and fit in his locker, to be stashed out of sight.

And worse: His father would assume he'd be instantly addicted to cape wearing, feeling utterly indecent if he were to ever step out of the house without one. Julian would get a new cape each holiday and special occasion until the end of time.

All of this was so horribly out-of-date and old-fashioned. But Julian's father would be so disappointed if he didn't pick one.

Sandra pressed the button again, stopping the whizzing of all the garments. "Here, at Toxic Masculinity, we can serve all of your cape needs."

"What do I even really need a cape for?" Julian asked, somewhat pitifully, with only the slightest bit of whine, hoping this might soften his father a bit.

Sandra let out a shriek. "All men need capes! All of them!"

"But why?"

"Because all men are supposed to be heroes!"

"Say what?"

"Yes!"

"Since when?"

Sandra's face reflected pure horror. "That's the way it goes!" she insisted. "All men are supposed to be heroes."

Julian offered a smile and nod, hoping that this time around, it said, *Let's just forget the whole thing.*

It may have softened her a bit, but she didn't quit. She placed a hand on his arm and assured him, "But you get to choose what kind of hero you want to be!"

"Oh," Julian said. It was all he could come up with. It sounded pretty hollow and lame.

"Are you into swords?"

"Swords?" Julian gulped.

"If you are, you might want to check out the Zorro collection." She held up a black cape, shiny as a plastic trash bag.

"Um," Julian said.

"No? How about…" Sandra spun the rack. "Oooh! I know! You're young. You would be good with our *Marvel*-ous collection. Here's one in the Superman line." When she snatched this one from the rack, it was wrinkled and looked to be made of polyester.

"Superman?" Julian was horrified. What could he do that was super? He'd won the Spelling Bee in the third grade, but only at the regional level.

"Perhaps you're an athlete!"

"I kinda blew out my knee in football."

This brought a sparkle to Sandra's eyes as she pictured the drama of a young man sacrificing a complex hinge joint in order to secure his team's state championship win.

"He blew his knee out at tryouts," his father explained. He wasn't attempting to humiliate him, Julian knew. He was just trying to get Sandra on the right track.

Only, what *was* the right track?

"Not the wall-of-physical-strength type," Sandra said, understanding. "No worries! Still plenty of heroes left."

Julian had doubts.

"Have you had any run-ins with radioactive bugs?"

"Say what?"

"We have our accidental hero line here—you know, like Spider-Man, that sort of thing."

"Um," Julian said again.

"Are you technologically gifted?" she asked. "Do you like gadgets?"

"I can update my phone," Julian said.

"That probably means the Batman collection is out." Sandra tapped her front tooth, thinking.

"Wait," Julian said. "Did you say this is the *Marvel*-ous line? Aren't some of these characters DC?"

"Details, schmetails," Sandra grumbled.

"How about a romantic hero?" she asked, brightening again. "Our Prince Charming collection—"

"We have an antique one of those," his dad broke in. "It belonged to my father."

"Oh, those are so special," Sandra sighed.

"And it has vintage mud!" his father exclaimed.

"That makes it more valuable," Sandra assured him. "I bet you could get it on the *Antiques Roadshow*."

Julian felt his gag reflex kicking in. They *weren't* valuable; the bottom had fallen out of the cape market, just like Beanie Babies.

"What do you think?" Sandra asked Julian. "Prince Charming like your grandfather?" She held up a gold cape with fur trim.

"Um."

"You want to right wrongs! Like Robin Hood! Our Woodland Warrior collection—"

"Um."

"Guns! You must love guns. Men and guns go together like chocolate and peanut butter. We're trying out this new line. It's the Action Hero collection. Now, most action heroes are too busy kicking in doors and steering motorcycles to want anything to do with a cape, that's true. Capes tend to get tangled in their legs and trip them up. But here, at Toxic Masculinity, we are dedicated to getting all men in capes. Because as heroes, men…"

Julian started to panic. He didn't want a cape. He wasn't a hero. He didn't like guns and he didn't like whiskey and he was awkward around girls and he didn't know how to rescue anyone. He already knew (thanks to a rotten infection not all that long ago) that he wasn't going to ever be gifted anything with SUPER DAD on it. He liked hot dogs and his superpower was the smile and nod. He was not fancy or refined or confrontational.

Did that mean he was failing at this eighteen-and-officially-a-man business? What was his father going to think of him? How could he honestly believe that Julian should be here, getting a cape that announced he was the sort who would be able to fix the wrongs of the world, when he couldn't even fix any of the items in that box of busted odds and ends (lamps, various gaming devices, remote controls, a calculator) in his room?

Julian felt a tear coming.

"Oh, no," Sandra said. She shuddered and covered her mouth with her hands. "Don't do that. You can't *do that*."

But the tear rolled down his cheek anyway.

Sandra gasped, closing the curtains at the front of the store. "There," she said. "Now no one will have to see that." She dusted her palms off. "Where were we?" she asked Julian.

Julian looked about the store. There were no other shoppers. Only him—well, and some lonely looking guy in the back, searching through a stack of discount capes, muttering, "None of these fit anymore. Why are these all cut for young men?"

Julian tugged the curtains back open and glanced out the front window as a newspaper rolled down the street.

"Nobody seems to come here much these days, do they?"

Sandra was shocked. "It's just a slow day, that's all."

That wasn't true. The place had all the telltale signs of desertion: creaky old hardwood floors that gave a little underneath you with each step. Loud, clangy pipes under the ceiling. The walls were dark in spots with water damage. And it smelled bad. It smelled like dust and mold and things that were rotting. Julian knew that it wasn't just the building that was deteriorating, though; the capes themselves had been here so long, they were starting to decompose right on the hangers.

Julian had to end this charade. He had to show his father this was wrong. *There's no going back to relive your youth*, he wanted to say, *no matter how much you might like to.* He wanted to tell his dad that his definition of a real man was one who had the guts to accept himself for whatever he was. One who didn't spend his whole life trying to fit somebody *else's* definition (like that random guy in the back of the store, still sifting through that discount bin). Julian was going to be his own man, a man of his time and not his father's.

There was, he thought, only one way to do it. If this went the way he hoped, he and his father would be able to put all this behind them and head straight to The Hot Dog Noshery. Julian was already picturing his Chicago Dog. Heck, maybe after all this, he'd have three!

Sandra raised an eyebrow.

Julian smiled and nodded.

Sandra sighed with relief.

"Give me my cape, madam," Julian proclaimed.

Sandra perked. He figured she would. "Did we decide which collection?" she asked.

"It's up to you. I do trust you, kind lady."

"The way you just spoke has given me a great idea! From our Medieval collection. A *knight's cape*. I haven't had anyone request this in ages." She winked.

"See how it catches the light?" she asked. "You'll be a knight in shimmering cape."

"I don't think that's how it goes."

"Oh, but honey, we make our own sayings at Toxic Masculinity, and then we force the world to repeat them."

"How do we do that?"

"Why, that's what pure intimidation is for."

"I'm not the intimidation sort," Julian said, sounding more definitive than he had since he'd walked in the door.

"Once you have your cape, it becomes so much easier!" Sandra said.

"Um," Julian said.

Sandra wrapped the cape in white tissue paper and lovingly placed it in a box. "If you're not fully satisfied, just bring it back. Like your father said, sometimes, finding the right first cape can be a bit tricky."

"I think this one will be perfect," Julian said.

This time, Sandra was the one who nodded.

He leaned against the counter. "Can I have that light now?"

"Julian!" his father shouted.

But Julian tossed a look at his father. A look that asked, *I'm a man now, right? Isn't that what you said?*

His father relented wordlessly.

Sandra offered a cigarette and lit it.

Julian inhaled and coughed, feeling like a demonic creature had invaded his lungs.

"Smooth, eh?" Sandra asked.

"Um," Julian said, between hacks and snorts.

Once Julian's lungs began to feel as though they belonged to him again, he ran straight outside. He ripped the cape out of the box, and he carried it to a nearby dumpster. He pulled the cigarette from his lips and held it to the bottom of the cape.

It caught fire quickly. Turns out, knight's capes are extremely flammable.

Julian tossed it.

You know where this is going.

It landed in the dumpster. The flame jumped from the cape to dance on all the rest of the trash inside.

Yes, that cape was a regular dumpster fire.

Julian turned to see what his father would say. In the distance, he could already hear the shriek of firetruck sirens. He hadn't expected them to be so quick about getting out to the old discotheque region, but Sandra'd probably been watching him through the front window. Poor Sandra, trying to preserve her job even after the rest of the world had moved on.

But would it hurt his father's feelings to finally see what Sandra wouldn't?

Julian sucked in a breath.

"A *dumpster fire!*" his father shouted. But not in fatherly disappointment. He said it the way you repeat the punchline of a joke, to show you got it.

Julian finally exhaled. As he'd hoped, a dumpster fire was a language that bridged the generations, telling his father everything he needed to say.

Really, when you thought about it, it was almost as good as a smile and nod.

His father began to applaud.

"You're *my* hero," his dad said.

Together, they ducked, to avoid the spray of the firetruck's hose.

The Flyover

In a land far, far away, there lived a middle-aged maiden named Jessica.

And she was at the airport.

Perhaps this detail of Jessica's whereabouts does not sound especially important to you, dear reader. No more important than if Jessica were at the gas station, or waiting for a public restroom, or reading labels in the chip and dip aisle at the Piggly Wiggly.

But remember, this is a land far, far away. And in lands far, far away, nothing works quite the same.

Not even airports.

Sure, this airport looked like any other. Large long-term parking section, plenty of people pushing carts full of luggage, lots of goodbyes being said. Multiple terminals, hangars, gates. This thing was enormous. Almost a city in itself. Just ask the stressed-out air traffic controllers up in the tower.

But the letters out front—KLNX—immediately distinguished it from any other airport.

At least, it did for the residents of this particular land.

You see, this airport catered entirely to a certain kind of person.

And it was quite clear that Jessica was one of them.

Why, you might ask?

Look at her there, sitting in her car, in a section of parking lot so painfully far from the entrance she'd need a map to get there. Watch her tilt her mirror.

Look at her tear-stained face. Mascara cascading.

She went to wipe her face clean but stopped, shaking her head at herself. Ah, what did it matter? The tears weren't over yet. Not even close.

Jessica gathered her plane ticket and her draggy-bag (one of those suitcases on wheels). She slammed the trunk of her car and began to limp across the lot.

She passed by the hordes of cacti, all in different stages of flowering. As luck would have it, her suitcase had an unsteady wheel that squeaked and squealed. And then it popped off, rolling all by itself across the pavement.

Jessica sighed. Ah, what did *this* matter? At least it would give her a chance to catch her breath for a moment next to the statue of Colonel Supreme Wing Commander Carter.

"He was something, wasn't he?" sniffed a fellow traveler.

"Yeah," Jessica muttered, staring up at the twenty-five-foot statue.

(Yes, twenty-five feet. Listen, the people of this land loved them some Colonel Carter.)

In fact, Colonel Supreme Wing Commander Carter was a figure of much lore in this far, far away land. *And* he was the reason this airport was not, in actuality, your average, run-of-the-mill airport.

It had happened long, long ago, as important events *always* happen in far, far away lands:

Colonel Supreme Wing Commander Carter lost his love. A sixteen-year-old Queen of the Night—*cactus*, that is. It might sound odd, getting a broken heart over a cactus, but Colonel Supreme Wing Commander Carter had spent more time in the air than on the ground, which was not exactly conducive to forming tight bonds with many human beings. Colonel Supreme Wing Commander Carter's one constant in his life was that cactus. Sure, she could be a bit prickly at times, but that Queen of the Night was always there, waiting to greet him upon his return.

Until one day, when he opened the door to his house, and found her all brown and shriveled.

"Nooooo!" he cried. How could this be? Cacti did not need frequent watering—which was why he had chosen one in the first place. She had shown no sign of illness or injury before he had left for that particular trip.

"How can you be dead?" he scolded her. But cacti are not exactly known for providing many lengthy explanations. Especially dead cacti.

And so Colonel Supreme Wing Commander Carter had taken to the skies again. This time, in the hopes that he could distract himself from his aching heart. He flew up and down and sideways. He flew loop-the-loops. He tilted one wing, then another.

And then something unexpected happened:

He found it. The direct path to the other side of grief.

I'm not joking. When he landed, he scratched his head. He wasn't hurting anymore, but it wasn't as though he'd forgotten his cactus, either. He could think back on all the times they'd had together and smile.

And he said it, the great proclamation all people made when they discovered something that could change the entirety of humankind:

"Huh."

He returned home and began shuttling people over—he wanted to share what he had discovered with everyone in the land. For a fee, of course. There is no great discovery that can't be shared for a small fee.

And it happened time and again: When they landed, his passengers (who had all lost something important to them) discovered that they, too, were on the other side of grief.

"Huh," Colonel Supreme Wing Commander Carter said, over and over again, witnessing the miraculous change in his passengers. Each change was simultaneously the same and yet also unique. Each passenger, after all, was getting over a unique loss. Often, the passengers joined in on this monosyllabic exclamation of awe and wonder. In fact, the plaque affixed to the base of that twenty-five-foot statue in this airport had that single syllable engraved upon it: "Huh!"

But the occasional small chartered flight of one or two passengers quickly didn't seem like quite enough. Using his life savings, Colonel Supreme Wing Commander Carter opened the KLNX Airport. Large commercial flights zipped straight over grief, which became known in the land as flyover country—the *heartland*, they frequently referred to it, because it did happen to be made up only of heartache. The kind of heartache no one would have to spend years and years slogging through.

"Just imagine what we'd be stuck with if there had never been a Colonel Supreme Wing Commander Carter!" Jessica's fellow traveler said.

Jessica nodded. These days, there had to be multiple flights leaving at multiple times each day, because there were just so many people needing to get to the same place. Why, this airport was the biggest and busiest in all the land. The whole parking lot was crammed full of cars, day and night. The website where people booked their flights was always crashing. Inside, the board behind the ticket counter with the flight schedule indicated it didn't matter which gate, which flight, which departure time you'd been assigned to. If you were a passenger leaving from this particular airport, you were trying to get to the other side of grief. The other side of loss. You were trying to get to happiness. Not the old happiness you had felt before (because that would mean you'd *erased* all memory of whatever it was you'd lost), but to a new sort of happiness that let you remember the good times with a smile.

"You brought luggage," her fellow traveler observed. All he had in his hand was an umbrella.

Jessica shrugged. "You never do know how it will be when you get there. To the other side."

"You mean you might not want to come back."

It happened that way, sometimes. Everyone said you should never make any big life decisions after a major loss, while you were still reeling in pain. But once passengers descended their flights, they immediately knew what their next step should be. Some instantly took an Uber straight back home. Some wound up deciding to go back to school. Or opened a business. Took a year to bounce around Europe.

Never before had anyone had such clarity about their lives, not like they had on the other side of grief.

Thanks to Colonel Supreme Wing Commander Carter.

Jessica's fellow traveler offered a military-style salute to the statue.

And then he disappeared.

Jessica, meanwhile, chased down her wheel (located under a rather brutal cactus, which attacked her left hand as she reached to tug it free). She affixed it to her draggy bag. And then she began to limp across the parking lot once more.

Inside, a voice boomed on the loudspeaker: "Now boarding for the 11:15 to The Other Side of Grief at Gate 4." And, "Also boarding for the 11:20 to The Other Side of Grief at Gate 9."

Jessica bypassed the vending machines that offered a wide assortment of facial tissues. She limped to the counter where she flashed her ticket.

"Thank you," the counter check-in person said, offering a polite smile. "Your pain attendant will be with you soon." He pointed Jessica to an empty seat.

She flopped into it.

And she promptly began to fidget. She bit her nails. And her lip. She tugged her sleeves over her hands. And then she couldn't hold it back anymore. She began to cry.

Yes, Jessica was bawling. I'm sure we've all seen those cartoons of people crying, where their heads are cocked back and their mouths are open and tears act like sprinklers spewing out everywhere.

Yeah. That's pretty much what Jessica looked like.

Everyone in the airport was doing some sort of crying. Some had red puffy faces, and others had damp handkerchiefs that they kept wringing out, and still others kept flicking away tears.

But Jessica?

Good grief. Sprinklers. Waterworks everywhere.

Olivia sighed. As soon as Jessica had started in with the shrieking and sobbing, she'd hoped the outburst would be short-lived. But it didn't look like that was going to happen. Olivia hadn't seen a case quite as bad as Jessica's since she got this job six months ago.

The bawling and the wailing—oh, the wailing! It was that awful vocal crying, like a baby.

Olivia got herself together. She checked her uniform in the full-length mirror beside the ticket counter. She straightened the silk scarf tied at the base of her neck, adjusted her hat, and slathered on a fresh coat of red lipstick.

And then she clicked her heels toward Jessica.

"Ma'am?"

Jessica just kept bawling.

"Ma'am?" She touched Jessica's knee.

Jessica quit then. Sort of. She quit the screaming, anyway. She was still sniffing and trying to catch her breath. "Yeah?" She wiped her nose with the back of her hand.

"I'm Olivia. I'll be your pain attendant. Can I get you something from the cart?" She held a hand to the side and pointed out the contents like she was a model on *The Price Is Right*.

"Pain attendant," Jessica repeated.

"Yes. I'll be accompanying you on your flight."

Jessica's lip quivered. "You're sweet, but you're no replacement. You know how I *should* be accompanied on flights?" And the bawling started all over again.

Olivia sighed and sat in the empty seat beside Jessica. She leaned in to murmur, "I know it's awful."

"You don't—"

"I've been a pain attendant here for quite some time," Olivia lied.

At that, she thought she noticed Jessica scoff a bit. Did she still look like she was new to the job? Surely not. But it set Olivia a little off-kilter.

"Trust me," Olivia said. "I've seen plenty. Hundreds of people just like you."

"Like me?"

Olivia nodded. "People who've lost their life partners."

At this, Jessica threw her head back and bawled again.

Olivia took Jessica's hand. "I know what a shock it can be. Were you two together long?"

Jessica sniffed again. "Yes. Since college. We've been through so much together. Graduation. Getting my first job. Moves to three different states. We were together when my mother died—it was the only reason I was standing up at her funeral. We saw the Rolling Stones together. We even went to Paris!"

"Lots of life," Olivia commented.

"Yes. I'm not sure how I'll ever face the rest of my life all on my own."

"Oh, sweetie, that's not going to happen. You'll find love again."

"No! No, I won't. Not like that. Not ever."

Jessica curled into herself, kind of disappearing inside her oversized sweater.

Olivia frowned, looking into her cart. None of these items would actually fix a broken heart, but they could calm the ache a little. Tide her passengers over until they could all cross flyover country—the heartland, that is—and get to the other side.

Yes, once the passengers arrived, they'd be okay. But until then, sometimes, a little indulgence to soothe the soul could help. Olivia offered Jessica a tissue from a box branded with the KLNX logo, then rummaged through her drawers of chocolate bars, new lipsticks, scissors for new hairdos, sexy shoes, beard dye for the guys...She even had a freezer compartment for ice cream. Not to mention a mirror that could magically remove ten years. Somehow, rewinding the clock—even for a little while—could help some of her passengers.

She knew Philip, the senior pain attendant (and the attendant in charge of hiring, who had been responsible for giving Olivia this job) brought along liquor. Olivia had always considered that going too far. Maybe, she'd thought, Philip was spread a little thin because of all the work he also had to do interviewing potential new attendants. But now...

What was she going to offer that could possibly soothe Jessica? She had not seen someone so forlorn, maybe not ever.

She figured this was the exact reason why Philip used the booze.

Olivia caught Philip's eye and made a sipping motion with one of her hands. Then pointed to Jessica and rolled her eyes.

Philip nodded. He rustled around in his cart and came up with a pretty glass filled with something pink and icy.

"Here, sweetie," he said. "Frosé. It's frozen rosé. Try it and see if it doesn't make you feel like the trendiest little fireball ever. Who needs 'em, right? You're going to be fabulous all on your own."

Jessica took a sip.

Philip and Olivia held their breaths.

"I never thought we'd ever be apart," Jessica moaned. "Never." And then it was Bawling and Waterworks: The Sequel.

"Looks like *somebody* drew the short straw," Philip mumbled into Olivia's ear. "Whatever are you going to do with this poor thing?"

Olivia shook her head. She had no idea.

But just as Olivia was beginning to feel it was all somewhat hopeless, a fuzzy, low voice announced through the loudspeaker, "Jessica Small? Jessica Small, there is a visitor waiting for you near Gate 12."

"Who could possibly want to see me?" Jessica asked, her arms outstretched in sheer desperation.

"*You* know," came the loudspeaker's reply.

When she just sat there, confused, the loudspeaker exploded in an exasperated sigh. "The *lost and found* near Gate 12, to be exact."

Jessica's eyes darted back and forth. "It can't be," she muttered. "Is it possible?"

She continued to look about the airport, waiting for an answer.

"Good grief, girl," the loudspeaker roared. "Do I have to spell it out? Your long-lost love is back for you."

All the others in the airport looked to Jessica with a mix of envy and disdain. If love was going to come back for someone, their looks wanted to know, why didn't it come for one of them? Why Jessica? What was so special about her? The fellow traveler who had met up with Jessica in the parking lot to proclaim his undying admiration for Colonel Supreme Wing Commander Carter now glared at her like she had kicked his puppy.

Jessica gathered herself. She pushed her frosé back into Philip's hands and checked her makeup in her compact mirror. And she took off running. She ran straight toward Gate 12.

There it was. Even from a distance, she could already see it all clearly. Her love. Waiting for her.

Oh, it was something to be chosen by the love you thought you'd lost. To have that love proclaim that it couldn't keep away from *you*. Love was mutual. Your passion could go on and on...

Your heart didn't have to be broken anymore.

Jessica laughed and skipped, gleefully shredding her ticket as she ran. There was no need to have to travel to the other side of grief.

Her love was no longer lost.

"There you are!" Jessica cried. She opened her arms.

And scooped it up:

Yes, *it*.

Jessica's love—the love she had been mourning the loss of—was...

a yellow patent leather high heel.

Horribly out of date. Scuffed. Banged-up. With gobs of glue now holding the sole on.

"Is that woman serious?" Olivia asked, slamming her hands on her hips.

Jessica hugged the heel to her chest. "Oh, there you are! Now, we can go back to the way things were. We can go home." She slipped the yellow heel on over her bare foot.

Now that Olivia looked, she could tell Jessica's other foot had been wearing a yellow heel all along.

"What're you so huffy about?" Philip teased, nudging Olivia.

"How dare that Jessica try to take up a seat on one of our flights," Olivia grumbled.

"How dare she?" Philip repeated, laughing.

"Yes! How dare she. These seats on these planes are reserved for people with serious pain. They've lost loves. Big loves. Husbands. Wives. Parents. Children. Best friends. Not a—*shoe*."

"Oh, honey, please," Philip said. "Don't you know the greatest love affair most people have is with stuff?"

"Come again?"

"Sure! Haven't you ever lost a *thing* you loved?"

"Well, I—of course, but—"

"Heather over there," Philip said, pointing. "Lost her favorite jean jacket. Left it on a seat in a movie theater. By the time she realized what had happened and circled back to get it, it was gone. And Jaime," he said, pointing at a different woman, "lost her aunt's watch, the one she inherited. Sammy," he went on, pointing at a man in the back corner, "lost some vinyl in his last move. That one, apparently, really stung."

"Some old record?"

"Signed by Bowie."

"Ouch."

"Yeah. Even if it wasn't, though, music means something."

"You can get another album," Olivia reminded him.

"No you can't! How can you be so unsentimental? That particular album of his played during his first kiss to his first girlfriend back in high school, and it played while he learned to dance, and it had all the right scratches in all the right places, and you just don't replace that kind of thing."

Olivia's eyes began to tingle.

"What is it?"

"This is stupid!" Olivia shouted. "It's nothing! All of you!

You've lost your minds."

But instead of getting angry, the crowds simply crossed their arms over their chests and stared at her knowingly.

"Get over it! It's stuff! Your piece of loved—whatever— is everybody else's trash! Most of it has no value at all. A jean jacket? Are you serious? Get over it. Get...get..."

Olivia collapsed onto her knees.

The crowds moved all the chairs aside.

And then Olivia face-planted right there on the tile floor.

Her shoulders heaved.

Her body writhed as the tears flowed.

"What is it?" a voice asked.

Olivia popped her eyes open. Through her tears, she could make out a bright yellow pointed toe not an inch from her nose.

Jessica squatted and put her hand on Olivia's shoulder.

"I totaled my Camaro!" Olivia wailed. "Two weeks ago!"

"Aw, sweetie," Jessica said. "Had you two been together long?"

"Ten years! We'd been everywhere together!"

Jessica motioned for Philip to come closer.

"I was always cussing it out," Olivia said, "because it would slide around on everything—puddles and wet leaves and even plastic bags in parking lots. But it was a good little car. It got boys' attention and they were always coming to talk to me. An icebreaker, you know? It got me everywhere I needed to go. Really, deep down, I loved it. Poor Cammy."

"Cammy was its name?" Philip asked through a grin. He was enjoying this.

"Yes! Poor Cammy. It didn't deserve the way I treated her. I used to pound the steering wheel at stop lights and kick the door shut when my arms were full. I wish I'd been kinder to her. I wish I'd waxed her a time or two."

"Here," Jessica said, pulling Olivia to a sitting position.

"Here, you take my ticket. Or the pieces I shredded it into, anyway."

"And here, sweetie," Philip said, handing Olivia the frosé.

Jessica slipped Olivia's hat off her head and tugged the scarf from her neck.

They helped her get to the gate.

Once she was gone, Philip nudged Jessica. "That was good," he said.

"So I passed?" Jessica asked. For this much was true: Jessica had never actually been separated from her high heel. This whole thing had been a ruse. A way to get Olivia to finally admit that she was hurting. Mourning the loss of her Camaro.

"Youbetcha, you passed," Philip said. "Most elaborate interview of all time. You are officially hired." He put the airline hat on Jessica's head and tied the scarf around her neck.

"Thanks for playing along," he said. "I knew poor Olivia was in pain and suppressing it. When she first started work here, she was a perfect fit. Lately, though...Trust me, a few months ago, she never would have resorted so quickly to offering you booze. She just hasn't been the same. Some have such a hard time admitting they've been in the midst of a love affair with an inanimate object. It can be more shameful than an extramarital affair!"

The two leaned in toward each other and shared a laugh.

"You going to throw those away now?" he asked, staring down at her yellow heels.

Jessica blanched. "Nope."

"Those stories you told about those shoes were true?"

"Yep."

Philip nodded. "Well, *I'm* certainly going to do everything I can to ensure you always know where they are."

"Yeah?" Jessica asked, perking. She twisted first one ankle and then another, showing off her heels the way Olivia had shown off the items in her pain attendant cart a few minutes ago. "I think they're pretty snazzy, too."

"I don't *like* them," Philip said. "I think they're the most horrendous shoes on the planet."

"So—"

"So, if those shoes are lost, and you're out for the count, then I'm going to need a ticket. I can't lose *you*."

Jessica turned as bright as the yellow on her heels. "That's quite the compliment," she said. She could feel herself warming to her new boss. She could hardly believe it. She'd never had a job before that promised to actually be—well—fun. Somehow, she felt as though she'd engaged in a flyover of her own, right past the usual trial period of a new job.

Seeming to read her mind, Philip agreed, "Yes, I believe that if Colonel Supreme Wing Commander Carter were here today, he would have something to say about that."

He and Jessica looked at each other and they said it at the same time:

"Huh!"

To Be Frank

Frank was living the good life.

There was no "once upon a time" about it. "Once upon a time" implies this particular stretch had been somewhat temporary, or belonging to the past. Frank's good life was a permanent state.

That's what Frank thought. He went everywhere whistling.

Yes, Frank was living the good life. He was a rather good looking man, and not by subjective terms. He was handsome, the sort who did not have to work too hard to convince women to fall in love with him.

Women were always falling in love with him.

He had a great career. One of those magical careers in which he was moving constantly in a forty-five degree angle. Just when everyone in the office thought for sure he'd plateau—nope, he went right on ascending to new heights.

He had a fabulous house. And he made enough money to keep it in new furniture and fancy art.

Frank knew about wine and music. He was somewhat highbrow, and was also good at collecting valuable things. He had an antique gold watch that a jeweler once offered him fifteen grand for when he brought it in to be cleaned.

But it wasn't just about stuff or appearances with Frank.

That s.o.b. was also a lovely guy. He was funny and he was kind. He adopted stretches of highway and kept them clear of trash. He mentored young adults. He had personally rescued three dogs on the brink of starvation. He had also rescued an elderly couple who had nearly drowned when their car was carried away by a flood. He rescued a child who had run into the street after his ball and had nearly been hit by a Coca-Cola delivery truck. The man rescued a peacock who had escaped from the city zoo, for the love of Pete.

I'm not kidding. There are newspaper articles documenting it. The city once had a special black tie dinner honoring Frank: Rescuer of the Decade.

Yes, Frank was living the good life.

If you weren't Frank, you kind of wanted to punch him.

But then Frank would befriend you or take your dog for a walk while you were sick or recommend you for a raise. And then you'd go from wanting to punch him to wanting to punch anybody who ever crossed Frank.

See what I mean? Good. Life.

One morning, Frank awoke as usual. He hummed while he shaved and he shaved while his egg poached on the stove.

But a funny thing happened that day:

Frank's hand slipped. He nicked himself.

And then he had to scramble to stop the bleeding. By the time it finally tapered off, his egg was overdone. He had to cook another, which made him late. Which meant he backed out of his garage without looking.

The person he almost hit blared one long, annoyed honk.

Frank climbed out from behind the wheel. He smiled and waved an apology.

The driver of the other car was a woman. Frank's smile grew three times as wide. This would be easy to smooth over. In fact, he figured she was about to fall in love with him right there.

Only, she didn't. She called him a bunch of four-letter names. And then she flashed five different obscene hand gestures. And then she took off.

Frank couldn't understand. Nothing like this had happened to him before.

Things only got worse: He went to work, to find the contents of his entire office in three pre-packed moving boxes.

"Hey, thanks for everything, Frank," his boss said, patting him on the shoulder and leaving like this was all normal, just the kind of thing you did on a Thursday.

"Wait," Frank said. "That's it? We're done?"

"Yeah," his boss said, and turned away, like it was nothing.

Frank took his stuff outside. His back ached and his knees popped three times. Which was weird. His body never hurt. He was a specimen of fitness. Why, he had graced the cover of *Fit Guy* Magazine four times!

Outside, Frank put the boxes in his car. He felt like tearing his hair out. But when he looked at his reflection in the side mirror, he saw he didn't have a single strand left to pull. He was bald!

He also had a large liver spot on his left cheek and bags under his eyes. He hadn't noticed any of this as he'd shaved, but then again, the bathroom mirror had been awfully steamy.

"What's going on?" Frank howled.

"Heh. So it happened to you, too."

When Frank looked, he saw a shriveled old dried up stalk of a man. In a large felt hat, no less.

"What happened to me?" Frank asked.

"You're over the hill."

"What?"

"Sure. Look." The old man pointed.

When Frank turned, sure enough, there it was, just behind his shoulder: the top of the hill.

Frank was shocked.

"But everything was fine yesterday."

"That's how it always goes. One day, you're in your prime, and the next—" The old man gestured toward the hill, the crest of which was now behind Frank.

"What do I do now?" Frank asked. "My job doesn't want me, and my body doesn't feel like it used to and—" He gasped, remembering all at once the woman who had nearly obscene-gestured him into a coma earlier that morning. "Women don't want me!"

"Bit of a playboy, were you?" the old man asked.

Frank grimaced. "I always hated that word. But I've had my share of love affairs."

"That's over," the old man said.

"At least there's my house."

"Oh, yeah—it's dated."

"My house?"

"Yeah."

"Overnight?"

"Yep. The neighborhood is an undesirable location. Good luck selling it."

"Maybe I can pawn my watch."

"Nobody likes that stuff anymore. It lost all its value."

"Over—"

The old man was already nodding before Frank could get the rest of the word out.

"I can still mentor—"

"Mentor what? Your ways are all obsolete. Technology changed. Yes, overnight. It's why they forced you out. No one needs to learn from you anymore."

Frank was astounded.

"Well," the old man said, "I'd like to help, but you see, we all have to find our own way in this thing."

And he took off down the street.

Frank let out a few—or hundred or so—well-placed swears and obscene gestures of his own. He cursed his boss and his face and his job and technology and the world. Mostly, he cursed that hill and its dumb point, now over his shoulder. He cursed it for letting him feel like his whole life was going to be a forty-five degree angle. The truth was, it was only a forty-five degree angle until you got to the top.

And then it was a straight shot down.

Frank staggered, feeling lost. The city he had formerly conquered was now a different place.

As the sun set, Frank noticed a light at the end of the street he was on. He wandered closer. Why not? What else was there to do?

When he got close enough, he could see that it was a bar of some sort. With lots of singing and laughter bleeding out onto the sidewalk.

It sounded like it was probably lots of fun. But not for him. Fun was back there behind Frank, too. Behind his shoulder. On the other side of the hill.

The neon sign out front read: "Singles Night! Over-the-Hillers Only!"

Frank's stomach twisted. So this was what he was now relegated to. This was going to be awful. He really should have settled down when his mother told him to. Now, he was going to be a sad shell of his former self. A lonely, out-of-date shell.

Sure, anyone he'd married would have been over-the-hill eventually, too. But at least they'd be there together. At least they would have known each other in their prime. It would have changed things, Frank supposed, being with someone who knew that at one point, he was the kind of guy who got plaques and black tie dinners and was sucked up to.

As it was, Frank straightened his back, bracing himself,

and stepped into the club all by himself.

The women throughout were older—grandmotherly, of course—many of them slightly heavy. And yet, none of them had their feet on the ground. It made no sense. Heavy, but floating?

Frank got goosebumps as he wondered what this was all about. These women in here were levitating!

One of the women giggled, catching Frank's attention just before zipping high into the air, leaving a trail of silver sparkles in her wake. She pointed a silver stick at him.

"N—no, wait," Frank said, assuming what was about to happen would be bad. Really bad. Everything else that day had been. Maybe she was going to tase him or something.

Another stream of silver sparkles shot out of her stick—more forcefully, this time. Kind of like a garden hose when you stick your thumb in the end.

The sparkles spun above Frank's right hand. When they settled, Frank was not tased—or in pain—or in any way damaged. In fact, he was holding an old-fashioned.

"My favorite drink," he said. And, sadly, somewhat apropos today.

"I know. You were just wishing for one," the woman said, hovering closer to him.

"How did you know? What—who—"

"Gertrude," she said, sliding her hood back from the top of her head. She was quite a pleasant looking woman, with rosy cheeks and lips quick to spread into a smile.

"Are you—?" Frank wasn't even sure how to finish that question.

"I'm a fairy godmother. Or was, at one time. Now, I've gotten a bit long in the tooth, as they say. All the modern fairy godmothers are svelte—they look like Hooters waitresses, some of them!—and use holograms and other high-tech thingiemabobs, doohickies, and whatnots. No one likes plain old wands anymore.

I got forced out of my position. Over the hill."

"Me, too!" Frank exclaimed.

Gertrude leaned closer, cupping her mouth. "Would you like to know a secret?"

Frank's eyes swelled and he nodded.

"This whole place is filled with fairy godmothers. Retired, of course. Like me."

"Do you always come on singles night?"

"Do we! We invented it. I mean, nobody comes out to the retirement home where we all live. So we thought—if the people won't come to us, we'll come to the people. I'm sorry to say, though, that no one else seems to like the idea of a singles-for-the-over-the-hill night. So many people who have just had it happen to them—you can always tell them by the tears in their eyes and the dejected curl of their shoulders—walk right on by. None of them want to admit that they are, in fact, over the hill."

"So it's just me and—"

"—an entire room of fairy godmothers."

"Who can still make wishes come true?"

"We'd all like nothing more! Sure, a person's ways might get a little old-fashioned, but that doesn't mean you lose your touch, right? We've all been hoping for someone to step inside with a few wishes. I bet the girls here will all fall head-over-heels for the likes of you. Here they come now—look at them, all racing this way. Clawing at each other to be the first one at your side. You watch. They'll all offer you trial wishes to show you what they're capable of. Oh, how they'll all try to one-up each other, vying to get their hands on you."

Frank started to laugh. He laughed and laughed and laughed.

Frank was still living the good life.

Princess Karen & the Ogre

Karen was a princess in the Kingdom at the Bottom of the Sugar Bowl. Look, I know there've been a ton of stories in this thing about kingdoms, but *this* one you want to live in. More than any other. Trust me. In the Kingdom at the Bottom of the Sugar Bowl, whole pecan pies dropped like fruit from tree branches. Rivers ran thick and slow because they were filled with peach jam.

The only thing in the Kingdom at the Bottom of the Sugar Bowl that was *not* sweet was Karen. (Come on—you had to know that was coming.) In fact, Princess Karen was as sour as a dill pickle.

It all began when Karen was quite young. She raced out of her castle and found the children of the land playing in the frosting fields without her. It put a little bitter spot in her heart. As time went on, the bitterness spread. Kinda like how that liquid stuff in cooked vegetables can spread across a dinner plate. The bitterness spreading in Princess Karen was about as appetizing as that liquidy stuff from your green beans getting all over the bottom of your hamburger bun.

Throughout her childhood, Princess Karen could be heard

saying things like, "They'll be sorry they didn't ask *me* to play. I'll show them." Her anger was often as hot as a cup of cocoa.

And, you know, not as tasty.

It continued as she grew: "He'll be sorry he didn't ask *me* to the royal dance!"

And, later: "They'll be sorry they didn't want *me* to be the head of the Royal Company Limited Liability Enterprise!" It was, in fact, the main chorus of her life: *You'll be sorry, you'll be sorry.*

One day, halfway across the graham cracker drawbridge, Karen stopped, her feet screeching to a royal stop. Her latest chorus of *You'll be sorry, you'll be sorry* screeched to its own rather abrupt halt.

Her peach jam moat, which usually sparkled beautifully in the sun, was now more murky and green. It bubbled and churned like an upset stomach. This made her furious.

She needed a better look.

But when Karen leaned closer to the moat, she saw an ogre! A real ogre, with slimy green skin and yellow warts. An ogre with six eyes and a body that was a strange shape—he almost looked like some sort of weird slimy cucumber.

But, you know, a really threatening, creepy cucumber.

Karen let out a piercing scream, gathered her skirts, and ran off to the royal shopping mall.

(Look, this kingdom is in no way behind the times. This all took place years and years ago, in the era when even magical kingdoms had to have shopping malls with movie theaters and arcades and candy stores, if they truly wanted to be viable.)

There Princess Karen was, in a try-on room, huffing and puffing and attempting to exhale herself into a dress. "Whoever put these ruffles on didn't know what they were doing," she complained. "These things take up too much room."

She tugged and tugged, but that zipper wouldn't budge.

"That does it!" she shouted. "Who mismarked this dress? The size is clearly wrong. I've always been a royal size four-and-seven-tenths!"

She gave it one last try, fuming now—and there he was! In the mirror! The terrible ogre! All green and wet and awful. He had followed her.

Princess Karen stomped out of the dressing room, the dress still unzipped in the back, her index finger flying around, pointing in a rage at various salesclerks. She demanded, "I must see a manager! This is abominable! I am being chased in your store by an ogre!"

But when the manager appeared and asked where the ogre was, Karen glanced about to find there was no ogre. Only the people of the Kingdom at the Bottom of the Sugar Bowl staring back, their eyes as wide and round as Necco Wafers.

She huffed back into the try-on room, even angrier than before. And there! In the mirror! There he was again!

Princess Karen tried calling the royal police. "I am being harassed!" she shouted.

But, alas, the Chief of the Royal Police cupped his ear, to indicate he was hard of hearing.

"Going to math class?" he asked.

"You're going to refinance?"

"Going to collapse?"

"Like a good romance?"

"Need a new road map?"

"No!" Karen screeched. "No, no, no! I'm being threatened! I am a princess! I must be protected!"

"You're infected?" the Chief of the Royal Police asked.

"Feeling neglected?"

"Something happened unexpected?"

Now, between you, me, and the licorice-stick fencepost, the Chief of the Royal Police was *not* hard of hearing, only liked to make Karen's cheeks turn colors (he thought of the shade as aggravated cotton candy). He nearly giggled himself silly when he heard her scream, "Gah!"

After that guttural yawp of utter frustration—loud enough to rattle the candy cane fields—Princess Karen stomped back to the moat. And there he was! Clearly! The ogre! Karen guttural yawped for the second time in less than an hour, gathered her skirts, and ran back inside her castle.

She stared through the panes of her Pixy Stix window, her heart beating like she had just downed an entire fifty-pound bag of Skittles and washed it down with a bottle of maple syrup. (Listen, even in the Kingdom at the Bottom of the Sugar Bowl, you could wind up bouncing off the walls like a hyper child if you overindulged.)

The thing was, Princess Karen was afraid. There was probably not a single person in the entire kingdom as frightened as Karen. She was afraid of spiders. She was afraid of traffic and thunder and flying. She was afraid of public speaking. She was afraid of elevators and insects with wings. She was afraid of falling and dust and the number forty-two.

Princess Karen was also afraid of people—yes! People! It's a horrible thing being afraid of people. Heights, you can avoid. But people? They're everywhere!

Mostly, though, Princess Karen was afraid that she, the King's daughter and therefore the person in the kingdom with more advantages than anyone else, was the least deserving of those advantages.

And if *that* was true, Karen had often thought, what would the people of the Kingdom at the Bottom of the Sugar Bowl do when they caught on to this fact? (Which, you know, fed into the whole fear-of-people thing.)

Perhaps the ogre knew. All the more reason to get rid of him.

Time to involve the king.

"Father!" she cried. "Help! There's an ogre in the moat! Sound the alarm! Call the palace guard! We'll all be eaten!"

"An ogre?" the king asked. He held on to his gumdrop crown as he peered over the balcony. "There's nothing in that moat but jam."

Karen peeked over the edge herself. At the same time, the vile ogre reared his ugly head. "Look! There it is!"

"Karen, I am a busy king. I have no time to waste on your wild imagination."

The princess narrowed her eyes and stamped her foot.

"Fine," her father said. "If there is truly an ogre in our moat, you have my permission to get rid of him."

Princess Karen rushed to the royal printing office. Two hours later, four hundred butterscotch-colored flyers had been tacked with fresh honey to every storefront, tree trunk, awning, and mailbox in the kingdom.

"Reward!" the flyers promised. "He or she who captures the wretched ogre in Princess Karen's moat will receive her royal income for the month! The ogre is green, slimy, warty, and smells dreadful!"

(Princess Karen had never smelled the ogre, not once. But she could imagine the creature would have to smell every bit as bad as he looked.)

Karen paced the castle floor, anxious for help to arrive. Suddenly, she heard what she thought was a stampede of wild animals. Frightened, she peeked through the royal drapes, made of unfurled Fruit Roll-Ups.

"Oh, holy Pop Rocks!" she gasped.

Every person—young, old, and indecipherable—was racing toward the castle door knocker. Coming from the left, the right, north, and south. Parachuting down from the marshmallow clouds. Riding in on the backs of their Swedish Fish.

They waved her flyers and screamed as they pushed each other out of the way.

Princess Karen heaved the heavy castle door open and pointed an angry finger at the crowd. "Stay back!" she ordered.

"We've come for our reward," one particularly eager subject shouted.

"You can't have the reward," Karen growled. She stamped her foot and shook her head. "Not without the ogre! That's my rule!" Her temper tantrum caused her gumdrop crown to slip over one eye.

"But we do have the ogre," a little girl said. She pulled out a mirror and thrust it into Princess Karen's face.

Karen screamed. The ogre was in the mirror! All slimy and green and nasty. She thought she could even smell him. "That's not funny," she snapped.

"It's no joke, Princess Dill Pickle," a tiny voice piped up.

"Dill Pickle?" Karen repeated.

"It's what we all call you," came a voice from the back. "You're every bit as sour."

"And this is the way you look," came the little girl's voice again.

"It is not," Karen said. Her anger bubbled under her skin, threatening to scald her like too-hot molten lava cake. "I have beautiful golden locks and strawberry lips. I'll agree that the ogre in the moat does bear a striking resemblance to a large dill pickle. However, I am not green and slimy. I'll show you."

She tossed the girl's mirror aside and stepped to the edge of the moat. Of course—you already guessed it—instead of seeing herself, Karen saw the ogre.

"Go away!" she screamed at the nasty creature.

"Go away!" the ogre screamed back.

"Get out of here," Karen said, waving her arms.

"Get out of here," the ogre shouted, waving his own warty

arms.

Karen put her face in her hands. So did the ogre.

"What's happening to me?" Karen's voice trembled with fear. "Am I under some sort of magic spell?"

"Only the spell of your own anger," the king said softly.

"Have I looked this way before?"

Answers bubbled through the crowd:

"When your seat was too soft."

"When the wind was too breezy."

"When you didn't get the first bowl of chocolate porridge for lunch."

"When you weren't picked."

Princess Karen felt herself cracking at that last one. She glanced into the peach jam moat once more. The foul, nasty ogre still stared back at her.

Slowly, Karen's embarrassment began to cast a shadow on her anger, cooling it off. Just as slowly, the green began to fade from the ogre's skin. Her shoulders relaxed and her fists opened. The ogre's warts healed; his shape shifted, pulling this way and that; the slime melted. The ogre vanished, and in its place was Karen's own reflection.

"I—I had no idea," Karen said, touching her face.

"I don't have enough royal income to go around," she apologized to the mob, which was seeming far less mob-like at this point. More like people who had flocked to watch a concert or a drive-in movie or something really good—like salt water taffy pulling.

"That's okay," someone shouted. "As long as we never have to see that ogre again."

The crowd cheered in agreement.

The entire kingdom was far nicer to Karen from then on—mostly because they could rest assured that they would not be attacked for greeting her. And, as a bonus, Karen found that in the Kingdom at the Bottom of the Sugar Bowl, beauty was something that turned to liquid and leaked outward—like a lollipop that got left in a coat pocket and melted all over the outer wrapper.

Yes, sweetness made its way to the outside of a person, so that a truly kind person born with very few—say—traditionally pretty features would become more and more attractive, the more you talked to them. You could see them change, right in front of you.

It was, maybe, sweetness's greatest power.

Perhaps it *was* a bit of vanity that kept Karen being nice to people, once she realized that. But here was something really special: the more Karen interacted with the people of the kingdom, and the more she spread her kindness around, the more she felt she might actually deserve to be picked—for anything. A party or a movie night or a trip to the hand-dipped chocolate shop.

Funny, eh?

Forever after, everything really was sweet in the Kingdom at the Bottom of the Sugar Bowl—the pecan pie trees, the rivers of peach jam, and even the once sour-as-a-dill-pickle Princess Karen.

✳✳✳

Many years later, Princess Karen's great-great-granddaughter came to her to tell her a story she had heard.

Karen listened as the granddaughter spoke of a land where only leaves and fruit grew on trees, and the rivers were full of water and not peach jam. She claimed there were many, many Karens in this land, all behaving like a bunch of royal nincompoops. Behaving—well…the granddaughter tilted her eyes away as she explained that they were behaving just like

Karen herself had when she was younger. Collapsing on the floors of department stores and accosting people for having ugly curtains in their front windows (and, therefore, ruining the look of the whole neighborhood). Screeching at people for getting too close to them on the sidewalk or looking at them too long. These Karens were always threatening to call their own police.

Karen's great-great-granddaughter said there were magical devices called "smartphones" that allowed the people of this land to record these Karens and then post the videos on a kind of bulletin board that everyone could see, with the help of yet another magical device called a "laptop." It all worked like a kind of high-tech pond that reflected bad behavior back at every single Karen in the land.

And yet, the great-great-granddaughter claimed, none of these Karens saw themselves in it. They shook their heads at the poorly behaved *other* Karens, the ones unfortunate enough to be caught on tape, and just went on with their own bad behavior.

Princess Karen (who was actually Queen Karen at this point) giggled at the naïveté of her poor, young great-great-granddaughter. "Please. You believe this? A land with water in moats and fruit in trees? And princesses who *never* recognize their own bad behavior, even when it's reflected right at them? What kind of story is that?" she asked. "Totally unrealistic."

And she picked a slice of lemon chiffon from the nearby cake bush and ate it in three swift bites.

Once Upon a Punchline

1.

Once upon a time, in a magical metropolitan kingdom, Princess Rosy lived on the top floor of a high-rise tower in the Frog District. Oh, but don't start pitying the young maiden; she wasn't being held captive. She hadn't been banished to the tower by an evil queen seething with jealousy. Nor had she been betrothed to a prince who'd rejected her with the swift and unrelenting judgment of a Twitter troll.

No, Rosy had not befallen some grim fate. It just so happened that towers were part of life for all the princesses in this magical metropolitan kingdom. In this land, every father was a king, every wife a queen, every child a prince or princess. And upon her sixteenth birthday, each princess was placed in the safety of a glass-topped tower, where she was on display (either like a new pair of Louboutin shoes or baked goods about to expire, depending on your point of view).

Princes, by contrast, moved freely on the streets below. They were living their lives, exploring their interests and passions, driving too fast and drinking too much—until they grew tired of the constantly-dizzy feeling of thrill seeking, and happened to glance up at the myriad of princesses they could call their very own.

Princess Rosy had grown up being the perfect buddy for all the males in the land. She enjoyed professional wrestling matches and action movies. And while this made for fun conversation, shouted through the glass of her tower, so far, it had kept the princes from thinking of her as potential sunset material.

That's not to say Rosy didn't have plenty of company. Boys did return time and again to wave at our princess and shoot the breeze; she did, after all, have the friendliest face of any of the princesses in their glass towers. But, listen, Ronald McDonald was blessed with a friendly face, too, and did you ever hear of anyone scaling the side of a high-rise tower to proclaim their undying love for him?

Right.

As time passed, our princess busied herself by revisiting the stories that had been read aloud to her by the king when she was little—magnificent, awe-inspiring stories, illustrated in black and white, of riding off into the sunset, each princess with a prince by her side. She even revisited her favorite rom-com princesses, who, in two hours' time, always managed to snag their prince and carve a place for themselves on Success Avenue, all without smearing their Tom Ford Ultra Length Mascara.

It set her imagination spinning, and sent her scurrying to her looking glass to try out a variety of new hairdos that just might snag her a prince. Updos, milkmaid braids, even crimping! For nothing was off-limits, not for our eternally optimistic Rosy.

Yes, in Rosy's most private space—those inches between the rather pronounced ears she had inherited from her father—

she dreamed of the day when finally, she'd say something to a prince that would make him spew the kind of honest laughter that gave him stomach cramps and tears and even hiccups. And once he'd caught his breath, he'd announce, "Why, I have been searching everywhere for an unpolished heroine—the sort who could likely trip on every single pothole in the road, the sort who perhaps does not quite have her magical act together. And yet, maintains the ability (after a brief woe-is-me period) to put her latest misfortune behind her and trudge ahead, shaken but steadfast."

After all, no one in this particular kingdom was perfect. Surely one of these princes would be able to see his own foibles and know that the most important thing would be to find someone who could laugh through the road blocks and rough patches.

Right?

And yet, there our princess sat, day after day, elbows on knees, watching the busy streets below—and daydreaming.

As time passed, our princess grew infatuated with bridges. They were everywhere, arching high above the streets. Boys explored them, traveling by foot or winged chariots, while our princess began to imagine what the bridges felt like—were the surfaces rough or smooth? Did cold radiate up from them, bleed through the bottoms of the boys' shoes during the winter? Was the sun warmer on bridges than it was in her tower?

Most enticingly of all: when boys decided the bridges did not arch quite high enough, they simply added another layer. Overpasses crisscrossed back and forth, making the Frog District resemble a confused, random scribble drawing—not exactly the kind of thing that immediately brought to mind picture-perfect happily-ever-afters, but to each her own, eh?

Other princesses were summoned from their lofty perches by boys who often liked to point out (with their chests puffed and their voices artificially lowered) the bridges they had built on their own. Their chosen brides began decorating the structures with zeal, adding bridge skirts or entrance curtains or strategically placed faux throw rocks. Meanwhile, Princess Rosy's crown acquired a crooked slant, the anti-frizz styling product evaporated from her curly black hair, and she collected tomato stains on her glittering gown from all the deep dish pizzas she'd had delivered.

Princess Rosy began to notice that the last of the single boys (some of them oozing the same appeal as four-day-old fish cutlets in congealed lemon butter sauce) paused in their own journeys down various skyward-bound bridges to stare into the glass of her tower. At this point, they were no longer stopping to chat. Instead, they were smoothing their pompadours—which were enjoying a comeback in the Frog District—or tugging jockey shorts out of their cracks, or checking their teeth for pieces of spinach.

"What gives?" Rosy shouted, but no matter how loud she got, or how she waved her hands, the princes stopped even acknowledging she was there. Could they not see her? Had someone placed a curse on her somewhere along the way, turning the top of her tower into the one-way glass of interrogation rooms featured in the reruns of *CSI: Magical Kingdom* she watched on Hulu?

Surely, Rosy thought, there had to be a prince just like herself. One that the other princesses had rebuffed. Someone who did not seem like sunset material because he did not have royal six-pack abs and had no interest in perfecting the art of the humblebrag.

But if such a prince existed, was she supposed to just sit around on her rump hoping he'd walk by one day? At the rate they were going, they'd both be collecting their magical social security before that happened. And besides, after all that waiting, would either of them even recognize each other?

Beyond the glass, bridges arched increasingly higher into the inviting sky, curving upward and swooping back down, almost like fingers curling, beckoning her forward.

Our princess sighed, staring down at her own two feet, which happened to work just fine, thank you very much. And she finally asked herself, "What the freak am I waiting for?"

2.

And so our Princess Rosy officially put aside her favorite childhood stories. She closed the book on that part of her life, so to speak, and stepped away from her glass enclosure. She set out into the world, a bit disappointed to find she'd lost a few bars on her phone by descending her tower, but delighted to learn that the world on the opposite side of her glare-reducing glass was strikingly vibrant. Oh, the magical metropolitan kingdom had so many colors—nothing at all like those silly black and white illustrations!

Yes, our princess was also delighted to learn that those silly childhood stories had been wrong about something else: the metropolitan kingdom was not a place to judge princesses for being single, on her own, without a prince to take her by the arm. The land had thankfully moved on from the days when a king tossed his unwed embarrassment an old shoe to call home. (As awful as it sounds, in olden times, an unbetrothed offspring resided in a cast-aside work boot that provided a modicum of space for her cats, her books, and the hordes of her "children"— i.e. the piano students who came and went with great frequency, so many of them, she hardly knew where to cram them all.)

The kingdom had modernized with the times. Rosy had not been aware of this until she'd come down from the tower. But she'd clapped with delight when she'd found plenty of other princesses had forged the way ahead of Rosy, knocking down barriers and fracturing the Frog District's glass ceiling. So many others had agreed with her that waiting in the tops of family towers was actually as useless as wearing glass slippers (they chafe, in case you were wondering, creating blisters the size of ox testicles). And because of those women, there was no longer any judgment; these were not lesser princesses, damaged princesses. They had simply decided, like our own Rosy, that they wanted to walk across the bridges on their own, build their own lives.

To be completely candid, the single princesses in the kingdom could not be boiled down to any one type. In fact, while it was true that some princesses had never been married, it should also be noted that others had, in fact, become domestic queens only to gleefully toss their own kings aside, into gator-filled moats.

The happy-to-be-free women who had restored their "princess" status could often be found dancing down bridges in leotards while singing of the detriments of letting an unworthy prince put a ring on it, an action they frequently likened to being tagged for ownership—like the practice of ID-microchipping the royal family dog. The princesses who had fed their lesser halves to the sharp-toothed gators were far more antagonistic toward anything male; they often gleefully even squashed crickets whose chirp was in the bass range.

Rosy was shaking her head at one such heavy-footed display when she caught another princess shaking her head right along with her.

"Esperanza," the princess said, holding out her hand for Rosy to shake.

"I don't know about you," Esperanza said, "but I have no grudges against men. Why, my own royal family has plenty of not-half-bad princes. There still have to be more than just a few males out there who do, in fact, have an intrinsic value far greater than being gator food."

This warmed our Rosy's heart.

"Would you mind—" Rosy started.

"Showing you the way of the land?" Esperanza finished.

Rosy exhaled with relief. "I do have some money."

"Ah, yes," Esperanza said. "The We-Trust-You-to-Do-Your-Best Fund. We all have one. Provided by our somewhat disappointed families. Even now, they still like the idea of grandchildren. Or perhaps it's that they'd rather we have a partner. Someone else we can fall back on when the going gets less than smooth. At any rate—the fund. At least, to get started."

"It won't go on forever, then," Rosy said. "Family deposits into my trust fund, I mean."

Esperanza shook her head. "To be expected, really. But no worries. You'll be fine here in no time. I'll whip you into shape. If there's something you need to know that I don't, one of the other ladies will step in. That's the way it works. We got help, and we'll help you."

Rosy was grateful to have made a friend.

Following Esperanza's advice, Rosy wore sneakers (Air Diana was the name-brand of choice), and tore her gown to mid-calf for increased mobility, upcycling the extra fabric into a variety of projects: a coffee cozy, a headband to keep her hair out of her eyes, and—best of all—a fabric wallet to hold the wads of cash she'd be making on her own, thank you very much.

Esperanza introduced Rosy to a wide swath of never-betrothed women who had descended from their towers on their own. They were not useless ornaments. They were quite adept at turning giant fronds into rain shelters and snapping the necks of enchanted geese come dinnertime—the latter being a quality that some princes gravitated toward and others found unnerving. The mere neck-snapping sound made some blanch, touch their own Adam's apples and back away while muttering something along the lines of being better off French kissing one of the gators.

Not that the never-betrothed minded this reaction. The harsh sun reflecting off bridges gave single working princesses thicker skin as well, making them especially resistant to hurt feelings.

Our own princess began to stumble, though—she liked the enchanted geese, and frequently wound up feeding the birds her own foraged nut-and-berry suppers rather than roasting them. She could not master the ins and outs of erecting a frond-shelter (great galloping winged horses, it was a more complicated task than knitting without thumbs), and—worst of all—no matter how many princesses were kind to her, professing they liked her and wanted to help, Rosy just could not figure out how to acquire the mystical currency required for ultimate survival in her new surroundings.

Her We-Trust-You-to-Do-Your-Best Fund would dry up any day now.

By contrast, wealth accumulation seemed to be something most of the unbetrothed were disconcertingly good at. This stemmed, in part, from the fact that the always-single ladies were not in much of a rush to get to the often-touted sunset. It allowed them plenty of time to master their chosen professions.

Esperanza had herself established an entire chain of splendid chariot garages. Business seemed natural to her—but what of our own princess? Would Rosy ever belong to the world of plenty (or, at the very least, the world of the jubilant-to-know-where-next-month's-rent-was-coming-from), or would she simply struggle for the rest of her existence in the magical kingdom, living out the rest of her years in a hand-me-down cardboard box?

Every once in a while, the princesses would gather come evening to bid one of their own a fond farewell. They would applaud as a princess headed off into the sunset, finally. Always, it was a sign of some success: a fortune had been made, an industry upended, a true life partner found.

"What happens *after* they walk into the sunset?" Rosy'd tried to ask Esperanza during one such ceremony. She had to ask four times, so that Esperanza could hear her over the applause.

"No one knows for sure," Esperanza admitted.

"Then how do you know that it's a good thing to go through the sunset at all?" Rosy asked.

"Oh, we hear all the time from the girls who have made it there. They're sworn to secrecy about the details, but they assure us it's wonderful."

"So why delay it?"

"You don't want to wish your life away!" Esperanza exclaimed.

"Oh, well," Rosy said, a little embarrassed, "I mean, I know it's good to stay and, uh, you know. Get good at your job. Have time to become accomplished."

"It's not just that," Esperanza insisted. "It's the journey that's enjoyable. A book isn't nearly as good if you just read the first chapter and then flip to the last line. You have to know all the stuff in the middle, too.

"Besides," Esperanza went on, "while it's true that staying here does allow you to become an expert at your chosen line of work, you can't *get* to the sunset unless everything is in its place."

"You mean not everyone gets there?"

"No. Didn't you know that?" Esperanza asked.

Rosy shook her head.

"No, the sunset isn't guaranteed. You can't go with the wrong love match or without having done something to better the Frog District."

"Is that why the princesses are all so nice to the newbies like me?" Rosy asked.

"Maybe. A little. I guess. But it's not like we're all scoring sunset points helping other girls. Really, it just feels so nice to help someone. Doesn't it?" Esperanza asked.

By this point, though, the fellow princess had safely made it into the sunset, and the crowd was breaking up.

One day, beneath a sky threatening rain, a few princes stopped to witness Rosy's latest attempt at completing a frond-shelter. Whether married (officially the king of his own castle) or boastfully a bachelor to the magical grave, princes traveled in both neckties and packs, making sure to stop along the way for two-martini lunches and quick rounds of golf.

As Rosy's latest shelter collapsed beneath her efforts, the men all began to laugh. "We've been out here laboring beyond family castle walls for eons. How you once envied us, as you stared down from your glass-topped tower. Our own journey isn't as swell as you imagined, now, is it? Sometimes, freedom just plain stinks, doesn't it, princess?"

Rosy didn't think she would ever make it to the sunset. This wasn't any better than being in her family's tower. She grew so uncharacteristically upset, she plopped down on a grassy spot next to a bridge and started to bawl. So loudly, in fact, that all the frogs hopped out of the moat. (Gators no longer had a taste for frogs, not when they could eat cast-aside former-husbands—who, it was often said, tasted like bacon. This allowed for frogs and gators to live in a kind of one-eye-cracked-open-at-all-times harmony.)

The kingdom's frogs hopped straight toward our princess, ribbiting and jumping and doing a few song-and-dance numbers to make her smile.

And she did. Our sweet princess smiled. And chuckled.

And cheered for those silly frogs. Of course she did. Nothing had ever been so bad for Princess Rosy that she couldn't find a reason to laugh.

Not far away—just a block or so south, at a rather popular bodega—a prince stopped in the midst of his purchase of a breakfast sandwich and an iced tea to raise his head. He could make out a lovely sound. A musical laughter far prettier than any he had ever heard in his life.

Little did he know, he was listening to our Princess Rosy.

3.

"**H**ark!" Prince Kevin shouted. "Hark—I—I hear—"

But his voice cracked, which surprised him. And the surprising made him stumble. There he went, tripping over his feet and skinning his knee as he raced out of the bodega.

"Drat," Prince Kevin muttered, while everyone around him sighed and shook their heads.

"Never fear!" Prince Kevin proclaimed, and he fumbled all about him, searching for something that might help stop the bleeding.

Prince Kevin patted the pockets of the Nehru jacket he always wore, complete with a red sash around the waist and a family crest embroidered on the left breast pocket. The sash was a bit awkward—it was quite long, and anyone near the prince worried that the wheels of one of the many chariots in the magical metropolitan kingdom would tangle in the material and it would be the end of the prince, Isadora Duncan style.

Truly, though, it wasn't just the sash that was awkward—it was the prince himself. His royal glasses had a tendency to tumble down his nose, and he was an utterly miserable conversationalist. He tried to tell jokes, but his knock-knocks fell as flat as Neverland pancakes (a far less fluffier breakfast than Belgium waffles—in fact, they're closer to crepes, if you want to get technical about it).

"Here," a kind voice offered.

Prince Kevin abandoned the sash, looking up into Princess Rosy's face.

(Rosy had come to the bodega for some frog treats, to thank them for making her laugh again.)

She smiled, offering him some Band-Aids, freshly purchased in the bodega. In the Frog District, the shelves of bodegas were always full, and if you needed something bad enough, it would always show up out of nowhere, over on aisle seven. Look, it *was* a magical metropolitan kingdom.

"Hey, thanks," Prince Kevin said.

"Yeah, I've needed those myself a time or two hundred. Feels nice to be able to lend a helping hand to, well, *someone.*"

"Kevin."

"Rosy," she answered, shaking his outstretched hand.

"Who's that?" she asked, pointing at Kevin's companion. A dragon, to be exact. A real, live dragon who went with him everywhere. The dragon was properly green and lizardy; he'd long been housebroken and enjoyed nothing else quite like he enjoyed a good round of fetch-the-magical-scepter.

"That's Spot," Kevin said. "Spot is certified by the MKFCC."

"What's that?"

"The Magical Kingdom Fanciful Creatures Club, which is an earlier model for and operates under bylaws similar to the American Kennel Club."

"Oh, yeah?"

"Spot comes from a long line of show dragons. I was about to take him for a walk. Would you like to join us?"

"Would I!"

Rosy walked him back toward the section of the Frog District where she had only moments ago been attempting her latest frond-shelter. She wanted the other princesses to see she was absolutely capable of making her own friends. Why, she enjoyed action movies and professional wrestling! That made for sparkling conversation.

Just as she caught Esperanza's eye, Rosy reached out to scratch Spot's thigh.

Unfortunately, Spot was brachycephalic, which made his fire breathing horrifically unpredictable. (At night, he wore a mouth guard—not for teeth clenching, but to protect against fiery snorts brought on by nightmares.) At Rosy's touch, Spot let out a contented nose-sigh that accidentally torched nine princesses' frond-shelters all in one blow. And there it was, mere minutes before a downpour. No—mere seconds. That downpour was even closer now than it was when the princes were chuckling at Rosy's inability to get her own shelter put together.

Esperanza and company were now about to face homelessness in a rainstorm. Which meant they charged, ready to chase the prince and his pet out of the kingdom. Hell hath no fury like a woman scorched.

"Wait!" Rosy shouted. "It was as much my fault as anyone's. I'm sure Spot here will let you take shelter beneath his wings. If you run them out, you really will be caught in the rain."

The ladies relented just as the first drops started to fall. Spot opened his wings and kept them dry. This gave the ladies a soft spot toward Kevin and his dragon.

And Rosy's actions made a soft spot in Kevin's heart.

The soft spot made Kevin reach out for Rosy, taking her hand in his.

The reaching-out made a soft spot in our Rosy.

So basically, it was squishiness all around.

One of the older ladies began to shake her head at Rosy.

To be completely candid, Rosy did not immediately believe that this particular princess was directing her crabbiness at her. Princess Mona's face was perpetually downcast—she was as meme-worthy as Grumpy Cat—and her frowns had carved a myriad of wrinkles around her mouth and eyes. She was also not what anyone in the kingdom would have ever called "a real looker." She smoked imported cigars and kept a derringer in the folds of her glittery gold stockings.

"What's wrong with you?" Mona demanded. "Why this one?" She waved her cigar as our princess's companion slouched bashfully, allowing his glasses to tumble from his face and clatter to the ground. "The Prince of Klutz? The Baron of Bumbling? Don't tell me you have a fondness for heaps of ridiculous problems!"

But there was just something about this prince—he wasn't a braggart. He did not puff his chest out and point to all the beautiful bridges his family had made. He was softer, sweeter than the other princes. As they'd waited out the rainstorm, he'd told stories that had made the other princesses roll their eyes, but Rosy had belly laughed. And there was a glow underneath that Nehru jacket tied with the impossibly long red sash—not unlike E.T.'s heart.

Perhaps most importantly, his eyes twinkled when he looked at Rosy, indicating he sensed something special in our princess. Yes, special. Even though she had no business sense or any ability to make a frond-shelter. Even though, in her own way, she was every bit as much of a bumbler as the prince.

"You were going to travel these bridges on your own!" Mona shouted as she walked along behind the dragon, the prince, and our princess. "You weren't going to spend your life waiting around on a less-than-perfect specimen of mankind. What gives?"

Our princess flinched. In some ways, she wished she was more like Mona—she envied her crusty edges and her tough exterior, her *outta my way, I'm gonna take what I want* attitude—and it pinched a little to be taunted by her.

And yet, wasn't this exactly what Rosy had dreamed of, up there in her tower? Hadn't she come down, in part, to find a man like Prince Kevin? Someone just as imperfect as she was? Someone who knew they'd get through anything if they bumbled together? It didn't have to be mutually exclusive, did it—career or prince?

Rosy smiled at Kevin.

Kevin smiled at Rosy.

Soft, mushy spots expanded.

And so it was official. Princess Rosy and Prince Kevin were a thing. In the tradition of celebrity couple portmanteaus, they became known as (ahem) Kozy. Everywhere they went, the frogs who had once danced to comfort our princess in times of distress now skipped along beside Kozy as they walked, hand-in-hand, down various bridges.

Kozy also frequently took Spot to the Enchanted Park, which offered plenty of space to play scepter-fetch. The park had its share of ancient, sprawling trees (they made the redwoods in California look like saplings) where Spot could hike his leg to take a magical whiz. Here, the three were too happy to even walk, preferring to skip—even Spot, though it was difficult on his three-toed dragon feet.

(The frogs also took candid photos of the couple and sold them to various tabloid outlets, but that's neither here nor there.)

As Rosy and Kevin and Spot tiptoed through the tulips and skipped down the sidewalks, Rosy encountered still other princesses who began to make confessions to her:

They'd spent plenty of time feeling down. As much, some of them, as they'd once spent in their families' glass towers. They felt like they were working twice as hard as any prince for half as much.

That much was true—there was quite an income disparity in the magical metropolitan kingdom.

"I get lonely," they sighed, looking at Kevin and Spot with envy.

And another thing: they secretly wished there was some sort of shortcut to the sunset. It was always somewhere off in the distance, no matter how hard they worked, no matter what they achieved, no mater who they were with. It seemed perpetually out of reach.

Which gave Rosy quite the idea.

"Prince Kevin!" she hissed. And explained her vision: "The one bridge the magical metropolitan kingdom doesn't have is the most obvious of all: the one that leads straight to the edge of sunset! Direct access to the Land of Happy Endings! Why hasn't anyone in the Frog District ever thought of it before?"

Prince Kevin scratched his chin, considering.

"With your connections, and these plans," Rosy said, drawing the blueprints for the entire gilded bridge lickety-split, "we'd be rich! Set for life!"

"Why would a bridge make us rich?" Kevin wanted to know. Even with his family's extensive ties to the construction industry (they did, in fact, own the company that had built three of Esperanza's chariot garages), this portion of Rosy's plan seemed sketchy.

"Because we'd install a toll both! Of course we would. We couldn't let people just go for free. Not when it could make us so much money. We should charge an absolutely enormous sum, because princesses will only need to go once."

"Let's do it," Kevin said.

As they began to build, it became clear that Rosy did, in fact, have quite a talent. She was really good at bridge designing and building.

Whoulda thunk?

As they toiled, Kevin, Rosy, and Spot began to draw a not-insignificant crowd. At certain points, the crowd collectively *ooooh*ed and *aaaaahhh*ed like they were watching a fireworks display.

But when word got out where Rosy's bridge was headed, the princesses got royally perturbed. This was going against everything they'd tried to teach her about sunsets. Why, it would allow princesses to cheat, racing through to the sunset without bettering the Frog District at all. And while they were at it, what was the deal with that toll booth? Hadn't they helped her out of the goodness of their hearts? And now, instead of helping them, she was just going to take their money?

It seemed magnanimously selfish, honestly.

Halfway through the bridge's construction, Rosy got what her fellow princesses called "a little cocky." No one had ever been so inspired, she was quick to announce. No one had ever accomplished such a feat! (Even though the bridge was, in fact, still a work-in-progress, and not technically an accomplishment—not yet, anyway.)

Another single princess (known to be highly observant when it came to snoot-value matters) recognized the family crest on Prince Kevin's Nehru jacket. Vivian was her name, and she was herself especially good at business, having developed and patented the formula for Sweet Dreams—a concoction that, when tucked beneath a single lady's pillow at night, allowed her to wake refreshed and inspired and hopeful. Yes, Vivian knew, Prince Kevin was well-connected. He had money of his own. Plenty of it. Perhaps, Vivian thought, she did not want to be single anymore. Perhaps she could do even greater things than the already-incredible things she had long been up to, if she could legally affix his family crest to the back bumper of her hybrid spinning-wheel-slash-electric-powered pumpkin carriage.

Princess Rosy was far too busy with her bridge to notice her competition. If she had, she would have surely fallen victim to a rather dramatic fainting spell. Princess Vivian was, quite honestly, a svelte beauty who wore a Marilyn Monroe *Seven Year Itch* knockoff dress everywhere—even to the enchanted dentist—and hopscotched over the bewitching subway grates in order to…well, it didn't take a magical genius to figure out why. (Online, she was known by the handle @VaVaVoomVivian.)

Determined to put a kink in Rosy's plans (and snag some of Prince Kevin's attention), Vivian yanked a stone from the middle of the bridge, where the mortar was still wet.

The frond-dwelling princesses shrieked out various warnings. Even perturbed, they were still trying to help.

Not to be deterred, our princess simply shook her head and called out, "Oh, please! That stone doesn't matter. I needn't follow established rules of architecture. I've got talent!"

But Rosy did gather the loose stone. She reapplied magical mortar and slapped it back into place. "Spot!" she called. "Do your thing! Dry this mortar with your nice, warm breath!"

Just as he went to take an inhale, his nose started to itch.

Wouldn't you know it? @VaVaVoomVivian suddenly had an extra large bouquet of daisies in her hand.

(While lovely, daisies are full of pollen known to be highly irritating to dragons.)

To Princess Rosy's horror, Spot drew his head back and unleashed a horrific, bloodcurdling "ACHOO!"

The sneeze was accompanied by a long steady stream of pure dragon blaze. Fire completely enveloped her bridge in a matter of seconds.

As everyone in the Frog District began to cry out in a kind of collective horror, Mona (who had pushed her way to the front of the crowd) began to laugh. She laughed until her head full of gray finger waves came loose. She laughed until her knees started to buckle. She laughed so hard, it started to become contagious, and a few other nearby princesses started to giggle, too.

The bridge was turning to ash. Pieces still completely encased in fire were falling off, splashing in a rather loud string of "KERPLOP!"s into the gator-filled moat below. The crocodiles snapped, angry at being knocked in the head by various fragments of architectural salvage.

Rosy's hands flew to her forehead in a definite *oh, no!* fashion. How was it possible?

As the catastrophe mounted, our princess narrowed her eyes and sprang into action. She attacked Mona, wrestling her to the ground and yanking her derringer out of her garter. With no previous gun experience at all (other than those *CSI: Magical Kingdom* episodes she'd once watched incessantly in her family's glass tower), she aimed and shot a magical fire hydrant. It exploded, spewing glitter everywhere.

Look, we're dealing with a magical kingdom here. Were you really expecting *water* to extinguish fires? Yes, glitter put out this blaze, every bit as easily as a water balloon falling onto the Weber grill in your own backyard.

The entire kingdom hissed—from both a dying fire and sighs of relief.

Mona shook her head and pointed forlornly at the glass tower where Rosy had spent her mythical young adulthood. "You've caused enough trouble, girlie. Get back where you belong."

"Me?" Rosy asked. "Why me? She was the one who started it, bringing those daisies." She pointed at Vivian, who was acting like she was too busy checking her nails to respond.

"Did she?" Mona asked. "Or did you start it all by being so desperate to make a little cash, you'd gladly build a bridge that would take advantage of people who had only been kind to you?"

"But—ladies?" Rosy pleaded. "I put the fire out. Right?"

Princess Rosy looked out at the other princesses throughout the Frog District. But there was no helping her. Not this time.

Rosy had fallen out of favor. They'd have fed her to the gators, if they could.

Just as Vivian had hoped, Princess Rosy bid a bittersweet farewell to her prince and his dragon. It had been nice while it lasted. Weird, too, at times. But nice.

4.

Being back in her glass tower was doable—at first, anyway.

But since leaving her family castle, Princess Rosy had acquired a slew of magical nieces and nephews. They all gathered around the king's dining room table for Sunday feasts.

One Sunday, our princess watched the king wipe his blackbird pie from the corners of his mouth, send his grandsons out to play, and pull his granddaughters into his lap. He began to read the same picture books with the black and white illustrations that had entertained Rosy during her own childhood.

Quite simply, with a bit of life experience on her side, our princess was horrified by the fiction the girls were being fed along with their Goldilocks brand porridge.

Her royal siblings nodded in approval as the king read aloud from the book that claimed the world had no gray areas. In the magical kingdom, bad was a hundred percent black and good was a hundred percent white; but it didn't stop there. Bad wasn't just mischievous, those books declared—it was evil. Good wasn't just nice—it was as pure as the magical kingdom's first virginal snow of the season.

To add insult to mythical injury, those stupid stories claimed it was easy to detect evil. Yes, in *The World According to Out-and-Out Liars* (or so Rosy decided every single one of those picture books should have been titled), evil wore a mustache that curled up at both ends. Evil had hunched-over shoulders. It *cackled*, for the love of wicked stepsisters. Conversely, goodness had fair skin and wore a size two and had yellow hair that could be whipped into a fishtail side braid like nobody's business.

Yes, that was the line of mythical monkey malarkey the king spouted.

Only, nobody out there navigating bridges looked—or acted—like the characters in those silly picture books. Princess Esperanza had been great to begin with, but when Kevin showed up, she disappeared. What for? Had she been jealous of Kevin? Why? Where was she when Rosy got kicked out? Why hadn't she stood up for her? Wasn't not showing up for someone every bit as bad as attacking her? Was Esperanza a black hat or a white one?

Then again, Princess Rosy had herself been something of a villain, deciding to charge those princesses who had been nothing but good to her. She had gotten all wrapped up in herself and behaved selfishly. But deep down, she loved those princesses. She missed them. And she knew she'd had a lapse in judgment, but surely she was still one of the good ones. That was possible, wasn't it? To live a chapter as a jerk but still get back to being a decent character?

Wasn't Kevin bumbling his way through being a kind and lovely person? The sort who'd liked the sound of her laughter and had tried to stand by her and all her crazy ideas?

Wasn't Spot a white hat, even though he'd lit her bridge on fire? Hadn't it been an accident?

"What does this stupid story even mean?" Rosy bellowed. "I'm not a perfect size-two yellow-haired fair maiden. I have black hair—am I evil? Have you ever known anyone as bad as those books describe—or as good? It makes us all look like cartoons—or, worse yet, punchlines. Why are you reading this nonsense?"

"When you have female offspring," her brothers informed her, "you must give them dolls and hair ribbons and tell them these stories. It's tradition."

"But why continue reiterating utter garbage? None of it's true!" She continued shouting as new thoughts came to her: "If you make a mistake, is that evil? Are you not fair if you wear a size sixteen? Why are you telling these stories about sitting around and waiting for a prince to give you your life? Why make these girls feel less-than because they are not perfect? We're all imperfect! Every single prince is a bumbler in his own way, too. *Especially* after a two-martini lunch!"

Princess Rosy paced. "You have it all backward. Turned inside-out. Evil is invisible. And it doesn't exist on its own. It's part of every person who breathes magical air. It lives right alongside goodness, like conjoined twins sharing the same spleen. In order to understand good, you have to know a little of badness too. Don't you? Isn't it true that if you tried to cut the good and the bad apart, they'd both shrivel up like a couple of Shrinky Dinks?"

When the king only stared at her, bewildered by her outburst, she continued, "Why am *I* sitting around listening to this royal crap?"

The truth was, she missed her prince, blundering fool that he was. She missed Spot. Their imperfections had fit perfectly together. Far better, she knew, than Kevin would ever fit with that Vivian character—who was the traditional definition of "fair," and yet, had been nothing but conniving and mean. More than that: Prince Kevin had completely invaded her squishy inner places. She loved him. How about that? And she thought there was a very good chance he loved her too.

So *what* if Rosy's bridge had fallen? Was she only granted one chance in life?

Says who?

She did not want to spend the rest of her magical days watching reruns in her glass tower. She'd left once, and she'd do it again.

She wanted more.

And this time, she was going to go get it.

5.

And so our princess returned to the site of her fallen bridge. It broke her heart to see it all shattered and busted up.

She plopped down on the ground and began to weep.

Sure, a second try was poetic and admirable. But she had no idea where to get started. And besides, the rest of the princesses weren't so happy to see her again. She had messed the Frog District up big time. They didn't care that she was back, wanting to make good.

Sometimes, it went like that. People only had so much patience for other people's mishaps.

Seriously—most people had enough trouble with their own.

At the sound of Rosy's remorse-laden sniffles, the frogs hurried deep into the water, where (with the help of the gators), they collected a few of the stones that had fallen into the moat. They brought them to the princess, scooting them close with their noses.

"Think I should try again, eh? I'm not sure. Suddenly, this feels like a big mistake. Maybe I shouldn't have come."

What was she to do?

Trumpets blared. Dragon feet (which sounded remarkably like hooves) clattered her way.

"Princess Rosy!" came a shout.

Rosy raised her tear-stained face in time to see Prince Kevin arrive, perched high on a dragon saddle. He tugged on the reins, asking Spot to stop. He raised his hand in a kind of *ta-da!* fashion, knocking his glasses off his face. The trumpets blew a few sour notes, winding the formerly triumphant song down to a pathetic fizzle.

Prince Kevin cleared his throat. "That didn't go the way I wanted," he admitted.

"Join the freaking club," Rosy responded.

"I was going to fly in to save you."

"That's the opposite of what I want."

Prince Kevin looked sad and dejected. But Rosy hadn't meant that she didn't want him. That wasn't it at all.

Princess Rosy picked up Kevin's glasses.

"Thanks," Kevin grumbled as she stood on her tiptoes to hand them over (Kevin was still sitting on Spot's back, after all).

As he slid them on, Rosy stroked Spot's neck. "He's an awfully nice dragon," she said.

"I've always thought so."

Rosy sighed. She swore she could see Spot's eyes begging her to just *tell Kevin already*.

"Would you like to know what the opposite of you saving me is?" she asked Kevin.

"You doing it on your own."

"No, you royal dope. It's me and another someone floundering through it all together. Me picking up your glasses when they fall off and you helping me with the frond-shelters. Being strong in each other's weak places."

"I can do that," Prince Kevin said softly.

"What about Vivian?" Rosy asked.

"She was a bit too vava for me. I missed you. Vivian never wanted to go to the park with Spot. And she never saw my quirks."

"Isn't that a good thing? Not seeing them?"

"Nope. You want someone who sees them and accepts you anyway. If they don't see it, they're not paying attention. You don't want someone who isn't paying attention. Fairy tales do romances such a disservice."

"Do they?" Rosy asked. She was getting a kick out of this, considering that tirade she'd had back at her father's castle. Besides that, Kevin was making good conversation! Maybe she really did bring out the best in him.

"Yeah," Kevin said. "They teach girls to look in mirrors. So many of them never learn to look the other direction. It seemed, for a while there, that you were different. I'd hoped, anyway."

Rosy kissed Kevin's cheek. She dusted herself off and declared, "Time to get to work."

"Are you sure?" Kevin asked. "I mean, the whole idea was kind of harebrained, wasn't it?"

"Not the whole idea," Rosy said. "Just the toll booth. There never should have been a toll booth."

"So you still want to build a bridge? Where to?"

"Straight to the sunset," Rosy said. "Like we'd planned."

Prince Kevin scratched his head.

"Here's the thing," Rosy said. "I know that together, if we finish the bridge, I'll be able to leave the Frog District better than I left it. And I know you're it."

"It?" Kevin asked. "Like what? Like *tag, you're it?*"

"No," Rosy chuckled. "It. My one true love. Would you, Prince Kevin, like to ride into the sunset with me?"

Spot tilted his head.

Soft spots spread all through them.

Kevin reached for Rosy.

And he kissed her.

Well—he missed, and he kissed her chin. But then he got it together and he kissed her on the lips. "I accept," he said. "And I think it's royally cool that you proposed to me."

"Okay," Rosy said, as Spot wiped a tear from his eye. "*Now*, it's time to get to work. And trust me when I say—" (for this part, her face was pointed at the frogs, but really, she was saying this to anyone who would listen—including any higher power who happened to be in the neighborhood), "I need all the help I can get."

Spot jumped at the chance to come to Rosy's aid. He was glad to help the frogs fetch the last of the stones from the water, considering he'd had quite the hand (or was that snout?) in the whole bridge-destroying business.

Kevin immediately set to work himself. (And, okay, so he tripped on his sash and fell on his face in his rush, but so what?)

Our princess began to notice something special about the stones Kevin's family had helped her get on discount: they were engraved with random words.

"Why did I not notice this when we were building the first time?" she asked Prince Kevin.

Kevin only shrugged.

But Rosy knew the truth: she had gotten too wrapped up in herself and her newfound "talent" to notice much of anything. She felt pretty dang rotten about that.

Now, Rosy realized that she could place the stones in her bridge in any order she wanted. What she built would tell the world something.

"What do we want it to say?" she asked Kevin.

At first, Rosy and Kevin began to adhere only the prettiest stones to each other, all of which bore lovely adjectives describing the happiness they felt as they began this new project.

The prince dangled from his long sash to help attach the stones in the hardest-to-reach places. Spot used his warm exhales to dry the mortar before any additional accidents or sabotages could occur.

The other princesses sat nearby, munching on finger sandwiches and admiring Rosy's chutzpah.

All but one, anyway. @VaVaVoomVivian pouted and stomped her feet, sending her skirt to billow up over her head (though no one paid any attention).

Mona, meanwhile, stood on the bridge railing, shaking her head. "Oh, God! This is awful! It's all so predictable and sweet, I want to gag!"

Our princess narrowed her eyes. "No, it's not! Happy endings are never guaranteed! That's another fairy tale lie!"

She returned to her project, toiling enthusiastically, glancing up every now and then in the expectation that the orange hues of sunset would soon begin to wash over the horizon right in front of her. But it never happened. *Gosh*, she told herself, *I must be making really great time, if the sun hasn't even begun to set.*

Eventually, she became aware of a warmth washing across the side of her face. Turning in the direction of the radiating heat, she saw, with utter horror, the telltale orange hues. "What *is* that? That can't be the sunset, can it?"

Prince Kevin began to chew nervously on his long sash. Rosy snatched it out of his mouth. "Spill it!"

"I—forgot to tell you," the prince admitted sheepishly. "While you were gone, the princesses all elected to pass Magical Daylight Savings Time."

"I don't understand—the sun sets later?"

"In a different place, actually. This would allow them more flattering light. Sunset, they all said, can be as harsh as a fluorescent light in a swimsuit dressing room. Moving the sun preserves the flattering light longer."

"So our bridge is going in the wrong direction."

"I've messed everything up for us," Prince Kevin groaned.

"No, you haven't—*we* haven't." The princess stopped to search through the stones. "Come on—we only need to put a bend in the bridge. A slight detour. Find the verbs. Lots and lots of verbs. We can still make it to the sunset. But we've got to get a move on."

6.

With the last stone firmly in place, our princess sighed contentedly. She squeezed her prince's hand. A new closeness existed between them, formed from having shared a goal. Created something together.

"*Is* this awfully predictable?" Prince Kevin asked.

Our princess jumped, nervous sweat breaking out across her forehead. Because wasn't being predictable one of the worst things in the world? Worse, even, than having bad breath or being mean.

"Of course not." Our princess threw her shoulders back with assurance. Because she had developed a theory about sunsets.

She whistled for Spot, motioning for him to hurry up and join them. And then she locked the gate behind his long green tail. Yes, now the toll-booth-less bridge had a gate with a lock nearly as big the old glass top on her childhood tower.

Glancing down, Rosy read the final stones in her bridge: "Thank you for taking my journey. Your own path is out there. With a prince, without a prince—who cares? Go find your own happy ending. Figure out what makes you feel alive, in the most joyful, corniest (because, come on—joy can be downright corny) way possible.

"But here's the thing: You cannot ride into the sunset by traveling somebody else's path, step for step. What's the fun in that, anyway? Happiness is forging your own way. That's why we all came down here to begin with. We were going to be our own women.

"Build your own bridge. You can look at mine and use it for inspiration. You can see how I put the stones together. You can tell which pieces are mine, and which pieces Kevin set. You should know that we had a dragon who helped us, breathing just enough fiery breath to dry that mortar as we went. Stay as long as you'd like. Spend the night! Come a hundred times! It's why I nixed that idea of a toll booth. This bridge is here to give you a roadmap of sorts.

"If you look close, you can even see where things started to go wrong. You can also tell where we got to giggling at it all. It can remind you to laugh when things get tough. But like I said before, you cannot take my exact path. And to keep the temptation at bay, I installed a locked gate.

"Expect the bridge you build to fall a couple—or, you know, maybe twelve—times as you're trying to figure it out. That's a bridge for you. They're frustrating that way. In short (too late), go get it, whatever 'it' is for you. Grab the starring role. Be the princess of your own fairy tale. And share it with somebody, be it a love-match or a friend or a royal cousin or a brachycephalic dragon. Grab life by the metaphorical jugular."

Good grief, she'd never expected to have so much to say. There at the end, her bridge had become as wide as a five-lane highway in order to get it all in.

With Spot in tow, our princess and her prince stepped off the bridge and into the warm orange hues. As Princess Rosy had predicted—or maybe it was hoped—the light was far too bright to allow them to stay long. They shielded their eyes with their hands and scurried forward quickly, anxious to put the glaring sunset hues behind them.

"Where are we now?" the prince asked.

Our princess jumped for joy, because her theory about sunsets had been ever-so-right. She pointed to a large, frog-green road sign marking the kingdom limits.

"Welcome!" the travelers' sign proclaimed. "You have arrived at a brand new *Once Upon a Time…*"

The Storyteller (Fin)

The storyteller closed his volume and said, "I hope those tales of mine were able to brighten your day."

Staring into the faces of his audience, he reconsidered his own words. "Oh, sure, look at you here. Spread out under trees, eating ice cream, playing fetch. All of you trying to act like you're doing just fine, having a nice day in the sunshine. Like you've got everything under control, no distractions needed."

The eyes before him got big. The storyteller knew them far too well.

"That's a lie," he said. Factually, though—no judgment about it. "You're not fooling anyone. You *are* seeking a distraction from the day-to-day. It's why you came out here in the first place. But you didn't find distraction, did you? Only a change of scenery.

"The truth is, dear former-children, what you really need is a new way of seeing things. And that can only be found in a story."

The storyteller adjusted the chin strap on his helmet, readying to take off again. He cracked a slight smile at the *please-don't-go* expressions plastered on many of the faces before him.

"You see," he went on, "like many forms of entertainment,

this was all rather pointed—and, as a result, my stories act a bit like a pick ax, chipping away at the life-and-death seriousness of it all.

"Because the thing is—what I have found to be the case—is that life is not oh-so-serious. We expect it to be. We want it to be full of meaning. We want our stories to be utterly unique. But really, life is absurd. Utterly and wholly absurd. Filled with clichés and repeating tropes. Your story and mine, they overlap in their preposterousness.

"Where you get in trouble, dear former-children, is in treating your adulthood with a seriousness it does not deserve.

"Oh, I know. You believe what you're going through is so important. We all do. It turns us into drama queens and kings. Later on, looking back, we seem more like fools. Regular court jesters!

"It's all outrageously silly. So the best thing to do is have a good laugh at it all. Even while the drama is unfolding before us."

He tucked his volume under an arm, placed his kazoo in his mouth, and took off on his skates, in the direction of new tales to add to his collection.

Days like these—days with a large audience in desperate need of stories like his—were his absolute favorite of all.

Holly Schindler

Holly Schindler is an author of books for readers of all ages. Her books have received starred reviews in PW and Booklist, and won both the silver medal in Foreword INDIES Book of the Year and the gold medal in the IPPY Awards. She is currently drinking too much coffee while writing her next book. Most likely, her constant companion, a Pekingese named Gus, is at her feet, tugging on her shoelace and trying to convince her to go for a walk.

Check out her other titles, get in touch, or subscribe to her comedy newsletter at:

hollyschindler.com